Strange and Curious
Unusual Newfoundland Stories

by Otto Kelland

Strange and Curious
Unusual Newfoundland Stories

by Otto Kelland

St. John's, Newfoundland
1997

Le Conseil des Arts | The Canada Council
du Canada | for the Arts

We acknowledge the support of The Canada Council for the Arts for our
publishing program.

We acknowledge the financial support of the Government of Canada through the Book
Publishing Industry Development Program (BPIDP) for our
publishing program.

The stories in this publication were previously published by Otto Kelland in *Strange
and Curious* (1986) ISBN 0-969275-90-0. Poems used in publication are taken from
Bow Wave published by Otto Kelland (1988) ISBN 0-969275-92-7

Cover by Maurice Fitzgerald
∞ Printed on acid-free paper

Published by
CREATIVE PUBLISHERS
an imprint of CREATIVE BOOK PUBLISHING
a division of Creative Printers and Publishers Limited
a PRINT ATLANTIC associated company
P.O. Box 8660, St. John's, Newfoundland and Labrador A1B 3T7

First printing November 1997
Second printing 2000
Third printing March 2003

Printed in Canada by PRINT ATLANTIC

National Library of Canada Cataloguing in Publication

Kelland, Otto P.
      Strange and curious
      Stories originally published in: Strange and curious (1986);
      Poems originally published in: Bow wave (1988).
      Includes bibliographical references.
      ISBN 1-895387-92-2

I. Newfoundland — Literary collections.   I. Title
II. Title: Bow wave.
PS8571.E4465S87   1997   C818'5409   C97-950241-1
PR9199.3.K414S87   1997

Contents

Author's Foreword

I would like to point out that back in the 1870s our police force was known as the Terra Nova Constabulary, and it held that title, at least until 1883, for in October of that year, my father resigned from the force and Inspector General Carty gave him this commendation in his own handwriting:

This is to certify that Constable Edgar Kelland has been a member of the Terra Nova Constabulary from October 1875 to October 1883. I wish to state that he has always discharged his duties to my entire satisfaction.

> *(sgd.) Paul Carty*
> *Inspector General*
> *Terra Nova Constabulary*

The present Chief of the Royal Newfoundland Constabulary (1986), Donald Randell, informed me that he can find no record as to when the change to Newfoundland Constabulary occurred. I do know, however, that when I joined the Force in 1924, the title then was definitely Newfoundland Constabulary.

In the stories embodying the experiences of the *Frightened Fisherman*, I have not used the correct names of the men who were involved for obvious reasons. In the remainder of the stories real names have been used.

In connection with the story, *Mystery of the Falling Shot*, I should mention that not only were the Pitmans and the two police officers present when those pesky pellets showered down, but several curious neighbours of the Pitmans always arrived at the residence to witness the bizarre occurrences. Several years ago I talked with George 'Jolly' Pitman and many other people as well who'd actually seen the shot fall. It was from Jolly and the others that I learned details of conversations which took place between members of the Pitman family and the policemen.

With regard to the *Springheel Jack* story, since he made his appearances in 1929, St. George's Field has shrunk so much that if the sprightly character were around today he wouldn't have very much room in which to do his cavorting. Back in those days St. George's Field was a football field and football matches, now known as soccer, took place there regularly. When Field Street was extended from Merrymeeting Road to Newtown Road it cut a large slice off the eastern end of the field. Then on the western side of that street extension a fairly large building, St. George's Homes, was erected for the purpose of accommodating senior citizens. That building, with the area known as St. George's Court at the western end of St. George's Homes, reduced the old field considerably. In addition, a large number of residences have been built along Merrymeeting Road which has just about wiped the old football field out of existence.

Whether the reader believes any or all of the stories contained in this volume, is up to the reader of course. But as food for thought, I take the liberty of setting down a quote from the great William Shakespeare, he wrote: There are more things in Heaven and Earth, Horatio, than are dreamt of in your philosophy.

In order to somewhat dispel monotony I have decided to include a few of my poems, some of which were written several years ago, others more recently.

Acknowledgements

I am deeply grateful for the generous and valuable assistance given me by the following people:

Mr. Hugh O'Neill, former Chief Magistrate of the Central District Court, St. John's

Mr. Donald Randell, Chief of the Royal Newfoundland Constabulary

Mr. Edward Coady, Deputy Chief of the Royal Newfoundland Constabulary

Superintendent B. M. Blachford of the Royal Canadian Mounted Police

Mr. Donald Morris of the Provincial Archives of Newfoundland

Mrs. Francis Ryan of the Provincial Archives of Newfoundland

Mr. Derrick Bussey of the Arts and Culture Reference Library, St. John's

Mrs. Betty Roland, Gloucester, Massachusetts

Dr. Bobbi Robertson, Secretary of the Newfoundland Historical Society

Mr. Michael Harrington, former Editor of *The Evening Telegram*

Mr. Ben Hansen, photographer, St. John's

Mrs. Iris Power, St. John's

Mr. Victor Clarke, Gloucester, Massachusetts

Mr. and Mrs. M. E. LaFond, East Gloucester, Massachusetts

Dr. William Hoyt, Rockport, Massachusetts

I thank also my daughter, Jocelyn, for editing and typing the original manuscript.

Mystery of the Falling Shot

During the 1890s, James Pitman of Lamaline on the Burin Peninsula held two government jobs at the same time. He was the Customs Collector and the Post Master. In addition, he was a Justice of the Peace and a notary public. One could assume therefore, with all those official duties surrounding him that Mr. Pitman was a very busy man.

When James Pitman was nineteen years of age he became the godfather of a baby girl, nineteen years later he married his godchild. There was absolutely nothing wrong with that as they were not blood relatives. From this happy union came a large family of male and female children.

To all appearances Mr. Pitman was pretty well to do. He lived in a large, comfortable home and his wife kept a maid who did the housework and most of the cooking. The dining room in this dwelling opened directly off the kitchen. One day, Mr. and Mrs. Pitman and their entire family were seated around the long dining room table prior to taking the midday meal. The maid bustled back and forth between the kitchen and the dining room setting down plates of fresh meat soup.

After grace had been said everyone picked up their spoons to begin the meal, when suddenly, a shower of shot commenced to fall all over the dining room with a goodly portion of it falling into the plates of the diners. This shot shower lasted for approximately two seconds, then ceased. At this unusual occurrence the family was shocked beyond belief. They all remained rooted to their chairs stiff as statues. But everyone did manage to turn their gaze ceilingward as it was from that direction the pellets seemed to have come. But the ceiling which had been painted every two years for over half a century was as smooth as glass, not even a knothole showed from which the shot could have poured down. The maid, Mary, a nineteen year old who had come out from her home in Fortune Bay a year earlier to enter service with the Pitmans, heard the shot falling and was now standing in the dining room doorway. To all appearances she was wide-eyed with wonder like everyone else.

Mr. Pitman was the first member of the family to become unfrozen. Reaching out rather gingerly and perhaps with a little fear, he gathered up about a dozen of the lead pellets. Every size shot invented up to that time, from the tiny number six to the husky buck was represented. Mr. Pitman gazed at the shot for a second, then remarked, "Well, they're real shot, alright, but how they fell or could be propelled into the room, I am at a loss to determine."

Of course the tasty soup was totally ruined. Mrs. Pitman who had by this time found her voice, instructed the maid to collect the soup plates and empty them. As a considerable amount of shot lay all over the dining room floor, on the sideboard and other furniture, Mr. Pitman ordered one of his sons to go and fetch George Pitman, a young relative who usually worked as a maintenance man around the James Pitman property.

George Pitman was in his twenties, a happy-go-lucky individual who never feared nor cared for anything that crept, crawled, or walked on two legs or four. His constant display of good humour earned him the nickname of Jolly.

When Jolly was told of the incident and had gotten the opportunity of eyeing the shot scattered around the room, he remarked to Mr. Pitman with a wide grin, "Gosh Skipper, you're some lucky to get all this shot for nuttin'. I always got to buy mine."

"George," replied the master of the house sternly, "I'm

not exactly in the mood to joke about this matter. So get a broom, sweep up this miserable stuff and throw it as far off in the barrisway as you can."

The barrisway was only a few yards from the Pitman residence. This miniature inland sea ran westward into the country for a mile. It was connected to the waters of the harbour by a gut and most of the houses on the west side of the harbour were built along its southern rim.

While George was busily engaged in sweeping up the shot his grin became broader than ever. He'd formed his own ideas as to where that lead would go and the bottom of the barrisway was not the place he had in mind.

As previously stated, all members of the family agreed that the shot appeared to fall straight down from the ceiling. The windows in the dining room were closed tight and none of the glass in them was shattered. So the pellets could not have come in via the windows. If it had come in through the only doorway leading to the dining room, then surely some of the diners would have seen the person throwing it. Furthermore, the maid who was in the kitchen at the time stated emphatically that there was no person in that room but herself.

News of the falling shot soon spread around the settlement and folks came in from all over to hear the story first hand and to offer their opinions as to where it came from. Several people termed it ghost shot, not because the shot itself was ghostly, it was very real, but because they figured that it had been delivered by a ghostly, unseen hand. None of their advice or opinions helped, however, for the very next day as the family was about to begin dinner, down came another shower of shot. Whereas the family's surprise and shock was not so severe as on the first day, the mysterious falling shot didn't aid anyone's nervous systems either. Once again each person in the room was prepared to swear that the missiles fell straight down from the ceiling. The delicious fresh meat stew which the maid had placed on the table moments before suffered the same fate as the soup of the previous day, it was totally ruined.

Mr. Pitman himself reasoned that twice was quite enough. He expressed the belief that some local prankster had discovered a way to propel that shot into his dining room without the culprit himself being seen. So he immediately dispatched a rather lengthy telegram to Inspector General John R. McCowan in St. John's advising him of the pesky shot and asking him for a police investigation. The inspector general in turn wired Constable Michael Fennessey, who was stationed at St. Lawrence twenty miles east of him to proceed to Lamaline immediately and to conduct an investigation.

The constable arrived at Lamaline at 12:30 p.m. the following day, just in time for dinner you might say. Immediately on his arrival the police officer went to the Pitman house and talked with Mr. and Mrs. Pitman and the other members of the family. Suddenly Mr. Pitman said, "Why Constable, you must be very hungry after that long drive. As dinner is ready you are certainly welcome to join us. We have corned beef and cabbage today."

"Thank you sir," replied the constable. "You have just named by favourite meal."

When everyone was seated the maid placed loaded plates in front of them. As they were about to begin the meal Mr. Pitman said, "Do you know, Constable, a number of our neighbours are calling that shot 'ghost shot'. What they actually mean is that the stuff is being thrown down by a ghost."

The hard boiled policeman was so amused at this statement that he threw back his head and laughed uproariously with his mouth wide open. "I certainly don't believe in ghos..os..ug...glug....!" Fennessey failed to complete the sentence and nobody present could fault him for that because his mouth was half full of shot. Yes siree Bob, just as the officer was in the act of guffawing at Mr. Pitman's remark about a ghostly miscreant, down came a shower of lead pellets, with the greatest amount of discomfort being suffered by the policeman. Fennessey spat out the shot into the palm of this hand gazing at it sadly for a second or two.

"I never thought I'd see the day when some character would commit an act like we've just witnessed in the presence of a uniformed member of the Constabulary," he said as he sprang to his feet. "If Mrs. Pitman and the girls would excuse us, I would like to talk to you, Mr. Pitman, privately."

Mr. Pitman agreed and they went out, entered another room and closed the door.

"Do you know," said the policeman, "I believe it's your serving girl, Mary, who has been throwing that shot around."

"But Constable," expostulated Mr. Pitman, "if she were guilty of those acts one of us would have seen her do it, as each time she entered the dining room with our meals she was in sight of everyone at the table."

"I'll tell you how she does it," replied the policeman knowingly. "She's a sleight of hand artist."

"A sleight of hand artist?" relied Mr. Pitman. "It seems to me that I have either heard or read about such people."

"Well sir," said the constable, "a friend of mine who worked in New York City some years ago told me that he'd attended shows put on by sleight of hand people and he found their performances to be truly amazing. For instance, they can do things like passing articles from one place to another and nobody in the audience, although they are looking at them, can see their hands move."

"But Constable," objected Mr. Pitman, "here we have a little teenage girl, the daughter of a fisherman in Fortune Bay who was never away from her home in her life until she came to work for us. Where could she have learned to practise sleight of hand and who could have been her teacher? I very much doubt if any person in her part of the country ever even heard of that art. No, I think that you are on the wrong track, Constable," finished Mr. Pitman.

"Well sir," replied the officer rather lamely, "she could have been born with the gift. And I think we should have her watched very closely by someone as she enters the dining room with the midday meal tomorrow. Is there any place in your kitchen where she can be watched without seeing the person detailed to keep her under surveillance?"

"As a matter of fact there is,"replied Mr. Pitman. "There's a tall cupboard on the far side of the kitchen right across from the stove and there's a knothole in the upper part of the door. From that cupboard through the knothole a person could not only observe the maid's movements around the stove, he would also have a clear view of the dining room doorway."

"Excellent," said the policeman. "Then sir, if you agree we will have somebody in that cupboard before midday tomorrow with the hope that the maid can be caught right in the middle of her shot throwing act."

Somewhat reluctantly Mr. Pitman agreed. Later Mrs. Pitman was taken into their confidence and they got her to agree to sending the maid away on a short message just before dinner time on the following day. Her absence of course would permit them to place an observer in the cupboard without her knowledge. The cupboard sleuth selected was George 'Jolly' Pitman.

Later, when the maid returned, she went about serving dinner filling a large tray with plates again containing soup. She advanced towards the dining room, but just before she reached the doorway down came another shower of shot. Jolly had seen her ladle out the soup, place the plates on the tray, pick up the tray and move toward the dining room. He was prepared to swear that she did not lay down the tray once she had picked it up and he said he could not see how she could have thrown the shot when both her hands were fully occupied in holding the heavy tray. So it seemed that the policeman's ideas that the maid had done it was out. Anyway, whoever or whatever was doing it, the shot showers kept coming down always at midday. Constable Fennessey was understandably embarrassed and exasperated; shot falling all around him, into his food and mouth and so far he had been unable to land the being responsible. Desperately he wired the inspector general telling him that the shot was still being dropped in the Pitman dining room and that he could find no clue as to the identity of the person or persons committing those most annoying acts.

Inspector General John R. McCowan was a former member of the Royal Ulster Constabulary. He had served on that force both in the mounted and infantry divisions. He was definitely a no-nonsense man. He could appreciate the nuisance and inconvenience the falling shot business was causing the Pitmans and he desired to see the culprit or culprits arrested and brought before a magistrate. So he called in his assistant chief or sub-inspector as that officer's title was known at the time: John Sullivan.

Mr. Sullivan was a Newfoundlander; he too was a non-nonsense man. He had risen in the ranks the hard way, joining the force as a constable and by conscientious devotion to duty he had worked his way to the number two position in the Constabulary. As an investigator he was considered without peer. He must have possessed excellent qualifications for on the death of Mr. McCowan he was appointed to the top post. He was the first Newfoundlander to acquire that position. His predecessors were four former members of the Royal Ulster Constabulary and Colonel Fawcett, a former British army officer.

The inspector general gave the sub-inspector a run down on the Pitman problem after which he instructed him, "Go up there Sullivan, and clean up that miserable mess, will you." He added, "I'm very disappointed with Constable Fennessey that he should day after day allow some local yokel to make such a monkey of him."

The super policeman finally arrived at Lamaline and immediately visited the Pitman residence where Constable Fennessey and Mr. Pitman filled him in with all the details relative to the falling shot incidents. Mr. Sullivan then took time out to deliver a rather stern reprimand to the constable for not having done more to come up with the guilty parties. He implied that things would change dramatically now that he had arrived on the scene.

When the zero hour arrived which was dinner hour, and also falling shot hour, the sub-inspector was invited to join the family in the meal. Once again soup was served. Mr. Sullivan picked up his spoon, took a couple of hefty slurps, then dusted his beard and mustache with a napkin, after which he complimented Mrs. Pitman on the fine quality of her soup. As the sub-inspector poised his spoon for dive number three, down came the shot. That the being responsible had no more respect for a high ranking officer than he did for a private constable was evidenced by the fact that Mr. Sullivan got most of the fallout in his soup, his beard and his hair. Constable Fennessey burst out laughing, Mr. Sullivan glared at his subordinate and the piercing look he gave him must have equalled the one that had appeared in the eyes of Julius Caesar at the moment the brutal Brutus rammed the shiv into his emperor. The sub-inspector appeared to have been struck dumb, but he did utter one word, "Unbelievable!"

Once again the maid was ordered to remove the lead loaded soup plates. She was then instructed to bring in the second course and she returned bearing a tray containing two beautifully roasted sea ducks. Meanwhile, Jolly had been sent for and he soon arrived to stand by until the meal was finished when he would sweep up the shot and supposedly throw it off into the barrisway. As Mr. Pitman was preparing to carve the birds, somebody at the table wondered if that shot was capable of killing ducks. Jolly, overhearing the remark shouted, "You can be durn sure it can, for them ducks you got on the table I killed this morning with none other than the so-called ghost shot. And real good stuff it is too. I knocked down five birds with a single load."

"What?" yelled Mr. Pitman. "You actually killed those ducks with that detestable stuff?"

"I sure did," replied Jolly.

"Then," said the head of the house, "I will not permit anyone to eat them." So he straightway ordered Mary to take away the ducks and burn them in the kitchen stove.

For three more days following the arrival of Mr. Sullivan the shot showers arrived right on time, during the midday meal, always with the whole family and the two policemen present. Then the leaden hail ceased and was never again repeated up to the time the old house was torn down some forty years later.

As for the sub-inspector, he came no nearer to solving the mystery than had the constable before him. One has to give Mr. Sullivan credit for trying his best. The idea of a ghostly hand delivering that shot was distasteful to him. So he had Constable Fennessey round up a half dozen or so teenage youths and young men who the Pitmans informed him had been known to commit mischievous acts and although he grilled those lads unmercifully, it got him exactly nowhere.

There are several whys, one where and one how connected with the falling shot incidents. Number one, why shot; number two, why the Pitman residence and no other dwelling; number three, why did the stuff always fall during the midday meal? Where could it have come from and how could it have been delivered without the person delivering it being seen? Sorry, no answers.

The Ball Ghost

The Anglican Cemetery at Lamaline runs parallel with the road leading along the north side of the harbour. As outport cemeteries go it is of fairly large size. When the first Anglicans arrived in that part of the country they selected this site for their first cemetery. They discovered also that the land was damp and boggy, so they criss-crossed the plot with several ditches in order to drain the land. On the roadside they dug an exceptionally deep ditch. The material from this ditch and from the others which they'd dug across the land was used to build an earthen bank all along the roadside to serve as a fence for their cemetery. This bank reached a height of approximately four feet. Later a pailing fence was erected on top of the bank. I mention the deep ditch, the earthen bank and the pailing fence because they will figure prominently at the conclusion of this story.

A few years prior to World War One, a young man was walking west on the north side of the harbour road. After he'd passed the eastern end of the cemetery he noticed a peculiar looking being coming toward him, approaching from the west. The time was 3:30 a.m., a morning of light mist. This creature as he described it appeared to him to be a large ball walking on two feet. He became very frightened and was about to turn around and run back from where he had come, when the object of his vision entered the cemetery gate and disappeared. The young man when relating his experience stated frankly, unashamedly, that as soon as the apparition disappeared inside the cemetery he took to his heels and never stopped running until he had burst through the door of his father's house.

When this story began circulating around, a number of people proclaimed that sure it was a ghost of some kind that the young fellow had seen, what else could it be they argued. It couldn't have been somebody taking a short cut through the cemetery to get home, because there wasn't any person who lived beyond the northern precincts of the burial ground and then its peculiar shape, like a ball walking on two feet.

The next person to see the unusual looking creature was a middle aged fisherman who lived on the north side, east of the cemetery and who was on his way to the west end to join his partner who was engaged with him in fishing operations. As he was approaching the cemetery gate he beheld Mr. Ghost himself walking towards him from the west.

"I got such a fright," he said, "that me feet froze right onto the ground. I wasn't able to move an inch. I tried to shout out, me mouth opened I guess, but I couldn't make a sound."

Then while he gazed in horror and fright, the ungainly looking creature entered the cemetery gateway and was lost to his view. Then the fisherman discovered that his feet had become unglued and that he could run, which he promptly did, never slackening speed until he reached his friend's house on the western end of the harbour. This man too, described the phantom as like a ball that walked on two feet. After the fisherman's story went the rounds, the terror received a name; he was called the 'Ball Ghost'. Three other young men at three different times encountered the Ball Ghost, who on sighting them promptly disappeared inside the cemetery. And those three like the first two, took to their heels and in all probability broke all speed records in reaching their homes.

The last person to see the notorious Ball Ghost was a young man named Richard Pitman. Dick, as he was more familiarly known, was over six feet tall, was broad shouldered and handsome. This night Dick had walked his girlfriend home to the community of Point-Au-Gaul, three miles east of Lamaline. When he was bidding his girl good night or rather good morning, she said, "Dick, I hope you don't meet up with that old Ball Ghost on your way passing the graveyard."

Dick replied, "I am going contrary to your wish; I hope I do meet up with him."

And he wasn't simply putting on an act of bravado to impress his girlfriend. He meant what he said. So Dick walked towards home. After he had passed the eastern end of the cemetery his attention was attracted by something moving up front of him; he quickened his pace somewhat and he finally could make out the spectre that had been the cause of terror for several people. The time was again around three thirty and the morning was once more shrouded by a light mist. Dick observed that the object walking towards him looked to him to be exactly as the other witnesses had described it. Like a ball walking on two feet. Anyway, the grotesque creature reached the graveyard gate several yards ahead of Dick and promptly darted through the opening and disappeared. Dick, without hesitation also entered the cemetery, an action which I freely admit I would not have dreamt of performing. Dick had in his pocket what was then known as the new fangled flashlight. Those electric torches had appeared in the stores in the French town of St. Pierre long before they had been ordered up from St. John's to be placed on sale in the stores in Lamaline. At the time of which I speak nearly every young man who had visited St. Pierre owned one.

Inside the cemetery a road led from the gate to the church which was and still is situated at the back section of the burial ground, approximately two hundred feet from the gate. Dick switched on his light and flashed it along this road but the bright beam showed no object on the road. Then he searched amongst the headstones and graves on both sides of the road but still found nothing. He was now beginning to think that there may be something to this ghost story after all. He then walked back towards the gate and arrived at the deep ditch referred to at the beginning of the story. He flashed his light along it; over the years bulrushes and weeds of every description had taken root and were growing in profusion there. Then his light showed him a long, white beard sticking up from between a cluster of weeds. White that is except for a rather dark brown stain which ran down the centre of its entire length, which meant that Dick had not only cornered the Ball Ghost, he'd also discovered a tobacco chewer.

Reaching down a powerful arm, Dick took a full turn of the long beard around his hand and yanked its owner to his feet. The gentleman with the beard, a man in his late sixties was known to everybody as Uncle Neddy; he lived on the north side of the harbour, a considerable distance east of the cemetery. When Dick pulled the old man up he noticed that he had been lying on a large brin bag that appeared to be very full.

"What have you got in the bag, Uncle Neddy?" Dick asked him.

"Fish me son, fish," replied the old man. Then he added, "It's stole fish at that b'y. Ya see," continued Uncle Neddy, "I always picked out misty mornin's to do me stealing and I always got the fish in the west end. I'm too honest a man to steal from me friends and neighbours on the north side or the east end. Ya see Dick, it's hard fer anyone to identify a man on a misty mornin'. When I met the first feller I give the fright to, I darted into the graveyard so as he wouldn't see who I was. I done the same thing to the second feller. Then of course with that big bag of fish across me neck and wit me arms circlin' out around it to hold it in place, it give a good appearance of a ball walkin' along. Then b'y, when I darted into the graveyard and dropped down in the ditch, the high bank and the fence hid me real good. Dick, me son," continued Uncle Neddy, "I got to take off me hat to ye fer havin' the guts to foller me in here. All the others who seed me never had the nerve to do what you done."

"Well, Uncle Neddy," replied Dick, "you must be pretty gutsy yourself lying down near all those dead people with bags of stolen fish. Now Uncle Neddy," Dick told him, "you take that fish back where you stole it from. And you're to do no more fish stealing, for if you do I'll tell everyone exactly who their Ball Ghost is."

Several years passed by before the story of Uncle Neddy's thievery leaked out.

The Richard Pitman who starred in this story joined the Newfoundland Regiment at the outbreak of World War One. He was one of the first five hundred, more popularly known as the Blue Putees. He died on the morning of July 1, 1916, when the Newfoundland Regiment was ordered over the top. I can well imagine with the type of courage Dick Pitman possessed nobody had to push him to answer the call for action.

He is also the same Richard Pitman whose name appears in the title of that very fine book by Joy B. Cave, *What Became of Corporal Pitman?*

When Big Tom Lost the Fight

Tom Warren was a mighty man
In strength and height and girth,
And time after time, yes, more than once,
Big Tom had proved his worth,
For he was stronger than an ox,
And handy with his fists,
And often brought his fishing boat
Safely through snow or mists,
He was liked by all the people,
Except when he'd get drunk,
Then 'twas peculiar how that genial man
Could act just like a skunk.

For when Tom was in the liquor,
He would act like a raging lion,
And his curses would reach the planets
From Mars up to Orion.
Then all would scatter from his path,
As his lips would utter smudge,
And 'twould seem that against all people
He held a mighty grudge.
One night Big Tom was drinkin'
'Twas the night 'fore Christmas Day.
And rum was flowing down his throat
Like a brook runs to the bay.

Now after he'd gotten loaded,
He commenced to curse and swear,
So lewd became his blasphemy
That he shocked all people there,
Then Uncle David Morgan
Who was eighty-three years old,
Said, "Tom, one of those days, me son
You may not be so bold.
For you've sold yourself to Satan
With every cursin' speech,

Yes, b'y you've really put yourself
Right close to him to reach."

"And when he comes to get you,
You will not be so brave."
Then Tom laughed long and loudly
And once more commenced to rave.
He shouted, "I fear no divil,
Whatever walked on sod,
For me, I'm big Tom Warren
I even don't fear God!"

Now the folks who'd heard Tom cursing
Were good, God-fearing men,
So when he'd finished boasting
He looked around him then,
And not a soul was in that room,
He stood there all alone,
For they'd been too scared to listen
To his unreligious tone.

And then he staggered from the bar,
Going out into the night,
For he had no companions
They all had taken flight.
Then he drunkenly decided
That he would head for home,
For he lived in another cove,
And had six miles to roam.
The road was dark and lonely
But Tom, he felt no fear,
He had walked that road 'bout twice a week
For nigh to twenty year.

And he'd often boasted of that, also
For not too many men,
Would walk that road alone at night,
For dread of Martin's Fen.
Now Martin's Fen was a gloomy place,

That stretched for half a mile,
And legend said 'twas haunted,
By something dark and vile.
But Tom was chuckling gleefully,
As he came up to this fen,
Then he challenged any bogish fiend,
To come out from his den.
"But I knows that your not comin',"
He shouted across the night,
"For there's neither man nor divil
Who can take me in a fight."

Then he started singing ribald songs,
With all his might and main,
When suddenly before him
Came the rattling of a chain,
And then it ran behind him
Then, again it ran before,
And a figure blocked his pathway
As broad as a double door.
Though Tom stood nearly six foot six,
And weighed three hundred pound,
The head of this being towered
Full twelve feet from the ground.

Then it grabbed ahold of Warren,
And spun him clean about,
Then felled him flat upon the ground
With a mighty, vicious clout.
But big Tom scrambled up again,
And remarked, "Now that was neat
B'y, you're the first to have ever knocked
Tom Warren off his feet."
Now Tom, he wasn't frightened,
Though he could easy tell,
That the monster he would have to fight
Was an agent up from hell.

Thought Tom, I really asked for it,
And I can blame none but me,
But I will not take backwater
From anything I see.
There you have to give Tom credit,
For his courage and cool nerve,
Although he knew what faced him,
From its path he would not swerve.
So they fought there until daybreak
Up and down that slimy bog,
And when the demon had vanished,
Tom lay beaten, like a dog.

It was there, some fishermen found him
Just shortly after six,
And judged by his appearance that,
He'd been whaled with many sticks,
They had found him there unconscious
And had tried to bring him to,
Every inch of his face and body
Was beaten black and blue.
Now then, they gazed about them,
And observed through the morning fog,
That alders and sod were torn up
Over, every foot of bog.

Then they took Tom to a doctor,
And notified Tom's wife,
And the doctor worked for three long days
Before he saved his life.
Tom finally came back to health,
And never drank again,
From lewd talk and from cursing
He always did abstain.
So when Tom would tell his story,
And he told it oft for years,
He'd say don't ever let God down
Or you'll shed bitter tears.

"For if I'd been a Christian man,
And livin' good and civil,
That night out on the lonely fen,
I would have beat that divil."
As it was my friends, you'll agree
Tom had a closish shave,
And the marks from that tough battle,
He carried to his grave.

Who Locked Up The Cops

The square at Fort Townshend during the 1930s was hemmed in as follows: On the north side by the old barracks that had at one time been occupied by soldiers of a British infantry regiment. On the east end by the Cental fire hall. On the south side by the office of the Inspector General of the Constabulary, the residence of the police Superintendent, the residence of Mr. George Coughlan, secretary to the Inspector General and by the stables of the mounted police. On the west end by a long old building that had evidently been erected to serve as a storage place for the regiment's spare equipment and supplies. During the 1920s and long into the 30s the northern end of this building was used by Mr. Thomas Pottle, the constabulary carpenter and general all around maintenance man. When Mr. Pottle was absent he always kept his carpenter shop under lock and key.

At some time in the past a partition had been erected across the building cutting off the carpenter shop and forming a separate room at its southern end. This room covered an area of approximately fourteen by twenty feet. It was in this room that Mr. Pottle kept such items as digging picks, shovels, crowbars, pickaxes, etc., which he found necessary to use from time to time in connection with his work. The carpenter never kept the door to this room locked. He possibly didn't think such a precaution necessary for as far as is known none of the implements mentioned above were ever stolen. At one time, probably during the occupation of the British soldiers, the door to this room had evidently been locked, for hanging on a short length of rather heavy chain was a huge and ancient padlock, the key of which according to the size of the keyhole must have been exceptionally large also.

Around the middle of September 1934, I was the police NCO, detailed to superintend night watch. The two constables who had been assigned to patrol the back section of the west end of town were Harry Symonds and Harold French, two fine, upstanding young men who took their duties seriously. One morning at two o'clock I reached the central fire hall; on entering I found Symonds and French who having finished their lunch were getting ready to depart to continue their patrol. As they were leaving I told them I would meet them later on. As the fireman on night guard, Mike Bennett, had the kettle boiled I decided to take my lunch also. The weather all through the night was of the nuisance type. There was very little wind but every half hour or so a dark cloud would rise up and a real downpour of rain would issue from it. Those showers only lasted four or five minutes, then it would remain fine until the next cloud appeared.

Shortly after Symonds and French left the fire hall, Mike Bennett and I heard one of those showers descend. Mike remarked to me that the policemen would get a wetting as they were not wearing their capes. I left Mike's company at twenty minutes to three. The Fort Townshend square was pitch black. Although several firemen and their families still occupied some of the residences in the old army barracks not a light showed from that quarter, no lights were visible from the Superintendent's residence or from Mr. Coughlan's house either. I had only gone a few steps from the fire hall when I heard two men apparently engaged in a bitter argument over by the mounted stables. One voice boomed deep and husky, while the other one was more high pitched. I, thinking that two of the mounted men had arrived in from late patrol and had a falling out over some matter, walked towards the sound of the angry voices. Although the voices were loud none of the words came clearly enough for me to understand. As I drew near the mounted stables the voices suddenly ceased. When I got closer, I yelled, "Hey, what the hell are you guys arguing about at this hour of the morning?"

I received no answer because there was no person present but me. It was then I realized that there were no lights on in the stables. Flashing my light on the door I observed that it was padlocked tight. Then a chilling thought occurred to me; could the men I'd heard arguing have been the ghosts of old soldiers renewing the altercations that they had engaged in during their lifetime? According to tradition several arguments took place between Captain Mark Rudkin and Ensign J. Philpot. Their disputes ended with a duel on a site near what is now Robinson's Hill. Ensign Philpot died as a result of that encounter.

Meanwhile, I walked out of there and continued along Harvey Road. I came up with Symonds and French by the C.L.B. Armoury. We chatted for a while, then Symonds said, "Sergeant, I know you're not going to believe this, but as you know a heavy shower of rain started just after we left the fire hall. We were right close to Tom Pottle's garden tools storage room when the rain came on, so knowing that the door to that place was always left unlocked and fearing that we'd be drenched to the skin, we darted into the building and closed the door.

"I," continued Symonds, "leaned right up against the door, while French stood a short distance away. In a few minutes the shower ended, so I said to Harold, 'Ok, let's go.' Then I got the surprise of my life for when I went to open the door it remained firmly closed and refused to budge.

"Then French tried it without success, then we both tried together, but still the door refused to open. Then, I cast about with my flashlight until I located a crowbar."

Here I will have to interrupt Symonds' story. This building had been constructed of studs, as the old timers called them. The studs were made from fairly large logs that had been flattened on four sides then were stuck on their ends and spiked securely above and below. Those studs were more than six inches thick. The old builders of that day sure believed in strength. The door in question had been made from two by six inch planks. It was equipped with three hinges and like the lock previously mentioned, they were massive and in good condition. However, the original screws which were used to fasten them in place had rusted away and carpenter Pottle instead of using new screws had secured them by using six inch nails which went firmly into the stud on one side and through the door on the other side. The nails of course went completely through the door and were clinched by Mr. Pottle.

Harry Symonds continued, "French and I tried to insert the sharpened end of the crowbar on the opening side of the door. We could have done it, but we realized that we would have to pry off at least two planks from the door in order for us to make an exit. But we knew that Mr. Pottle would not be very pleased to find his door partly demolished. So we changed tactics and went to work on the hinges on the stud side. We succeeded in withdrawing all six inch nails and so got the door open. We left the building by that side."

Naturally on emergence they flashed their lights on the other side of the door and were surprised and amazed to discover that the ancient lock on its chain had been brought across and had been fastened securely through the staple on the opposite side. Evidently imagining that I was skeptical of the story, both Symonds and French said together that if I went back with them, they would show me. So back we went to find the door somewhat askew, but with the old lock in place exactly as Harry Symonds had described it. We shook it hard several times, but it remained firmly locked.

When thinking about the case of the locked in policemen there is one vital factor that has to be considered. That is, whoever had brought the old lock across the length of its chain and hooked it through the staple on the opposite side, had to open it first by using a key and then relock it on the staple with the key. Even a self-locking lock would have to be opened with a key and these had not been invented when that old lock was manufactured.

I talked with Fire Superintendent Michael Codner a couple of days later and told him of the Symonds/French incident. He informed me that when he joined the fire department forty years earlier the key to that old lock had been missing; furthermore, he'd said men who were fifteen and twenty years senior to him told him the key had been missing when they joined the fire department.

The morning following the locking, carpenter Pottle was forced to sever the lock chain with a hacksaw before he could put his door in working order again. The old building containing the carpenter shop and the garden tools room, together with the mounted stables were demolished shortly after the incident described here occurred. This was done in order to provide space for a new police barracks. The old lock must have disappeared during the demolition process, and was never seen again.

You will recall that Harry Symonds stated that when he and French entered the building he'd leaned up against the door and had remained in that position until the time came for them to leave. Both Harry Symonds and Harold French possessed excellent hearing so one could imagine that Symonds at least would have heard a rattle from the chain or a grating sound when the hasp of the lock was passed through the staple, or a grinding noise caused by the turning of the key. He heard nothing.

Retired constables Harry Symonds and Harold French, now in their seventies and in excellent health, well remember that morning fifty-two years ago when some mysterious agency locked them in the old tool shed at Fort Townshend.

The Strange Creatures of Bonavista Bay

Charlie Blackwood, the genial owner-manager of the City Tire and Auto service station on Topsail Road, told me that one Saturday afternoon in August 1971, he and his cousin David Blackwood went on a bird hunting trip. They left Brookfield, Bonavista Bay, at 2:30 p.m. in a sturdy eighteen foot boat that was equipped with an outboard motor. Charlie was twenty-five years old at that time and his cousin was thirty-three.

I make mention of their ages to point out the fact that they could not be considered inexperienced youngsters. In fact, like most outport men, they had been using guns since they were teenagers. They were seasoned hunters and had had many years behind them of near brushes with injury and death, while venturing out on hunting expeditions.

Charlie said that they passed by Cabot Island and when they reached about three miles outside of it they encountered birds. During the next hour or so, they managed to secure two dozen, mostly turrs. Then they noticed that a heavy fog bank was rolling in toward them. So they decided the time was ripe for them to head home. They certainly had no desire to be caught out in dense fog, particularly if darkness should come down before they reached Brookfield.

David started the motor and steered towards land, but they had only gone a few yards when the fog engulfed them completely. They did not have a compass with them, so David was forced to run by his own judgement or by dead reckoning, as the old fishermen used to term it. Sometime later a hunk of land loomed up on their starboard side and by its contours both men were sure that it was Cabot Island. They continued on, then David decided to cut down their speed and it was fortunate that he did, for Charlie, who was up for'ard on lookout, sighted a braking rock dead ahead. But at the slow speed they were going David easily avoided it.

They continued on for another twenty minutes, then their engine developed trouble. It commenced to sputter, bark and slow up, finally it stopped altogether. David started to work on it. After about half an hour, he discovered the trouble and got it going again. While the motor had been inactive, the men noticed that a heavy tide was running, but because of not having a compass they were unable to tell in what direction it was heading. However, they knew that during the half hour, while the engine had been broken down, the tide, together with a light wind which as blowing in the same direction, must have driven their boat a considerable distance from where they had stopped.

David Blackwood hardly knew in what direction to point the boat. After he'd gotten the engine running, he made a decision and they carried on at slow speed. After a long time both men realized that if they had been steering the right course then they should have reached Brookfield or land near it. Now they were forced to admit that they were hopelessly astray.

Suddenly Charlie who was still up for'ard, shouted that he could discern land off their port bow. David cut the motor down to dead slow and eased the boat towards it. As they moved in closer they discovered what they were approaching was apparently a small island with a twelve foot high cliff running the length of it. As they got quite near the shore, they noticed a large number of big boulders piled up from the shoreline to the base of the cliff, probably forced ashore by ice over the years. Charlie suggested to David that as it would be dark very soon, they should land the boat and secure her there for the night. David agreed with the proposal. While he eased the boat shoreward Charlie coiled the painter and held it in his hand ready to jump ashore and make it fast when the craft grounded.

But before that occurred Charlie looked up towards the land and instantly spied standing on the cliff top, two of the strangest looking creatures he had ever beheld. They were standing with legs apart, arms at their sides and seemed to be peering down at the men in the boat. Charlie said to David, "Do you see what I see?"

"Yeah," replied David, "I see 'em, but what in the hell are they? I've never seen anything like them before."

"Neither have I. So don't ask me what they are."

Immediately both men decided not to land and secure the boat to that island. Having no idea what the creatures were or what harm they may cause, they reasoned that it would be safer to remain on the open water. But was it? That was a question the bird hunters asked each other later. The two creatures did not appear to be frightened or too disturbed over the presence of the two men in the boat. Before David started the motor, preparing to move off, the two figures walked slowly along the cliff, away from the Blackwoods, until they found an easy place to descend. Then they leaped from boulder to boulder until they reached the sea, where they promptly dived in and disappeared beneath the surface. Although David and Charlie watched closely for several minutes, the creatures did not reappear.

David started the motor and they moved away from the island. After steaming along slowly for a few minutes, the men noticed a large codnet set in the water. As it was nearly dark by this time, they decided to tie fast to it and await daylight. Then with considerable feelings of dread, Charlie and David held a discussion concerning the two strange, man-like figures they had seen.

David said, "If there's two of 'em, and that we know, there could be dozens more, and we both saw they can, apparently, live under water as well as on land."

"You know," added Charlie, "them two must have a father and mother or they wouldn't have turned up here in the first place. If they happen to be the kind of creatures that are inclined to attack us, our only hope is that their old man and old woman didn't produce a whole swarm of them. I say, that if they should happen to sneak up to our boat and attempt to board her, the only thing that is left for us to do is blast them with our guns as long as our ammunition holds out, after that I don't know what will happen."

His cousin finally agreed. So they loaded their double barrelled shotguns with Charlie taking up position in the bow while David remained aft.

Both Charlie and David told me that they put in a hell of a poor night. Sleep was out of the question.

"We were forced to remain on constant alert in case those two bastards we'd seen decided to pay us a visit. Fortunately there was only a light wind and no high seas running, while the August night wasn't very chilly. Anyway," continued David, "we were well clad, so suffered no discomfort that way. We weren't hungry either, because we'd brought along a good supply of sandwiches. We would have liked to brew a mug of tea, as we carried a small kettle with us and a kerosene torch. You know the kind that's called a flare-up. It had a large wick and you could boil a small kettle on it quickly, but we did not dare to use it as we feared that the light would attract those sons-of-guns to our boat. But I am very proud and happy to say that we saw no further signs of them."

"Shortly after daylight the wind hauled off from the northwest. This of course cleared away the fog in a hurry," said Charlie. "It was then we discovered that we were quite a distance to the northeast of where we should have been."

They started the motor and they arrived home without

mishap and just in time to prevent a search party from leaving port to locate them.

In describing the strange creatures, Charlie and David estimated them to be four and a half feet tall and very broad across the shoulders. The way Charlie put it, it could be just as easy to jump over them as walk around them, because they were that wide. Their arms and legs were short, and their heads appeared to be round. At that distance, one hundred feet, the men could not make out either nose nor eyes, but they could observe ears, shaped like human ears only much larger and sticking out from the sides of their heads.

Their bodies seemed to be covered with greyish coloured hair or fur. They had no distinct neck. What could be classed as a neck sloped right out and joined the shoulders. While they were watching, Charlie and David asserted the creatures never uttered a sound, no bark, no grunt, nor squeal.

Sometime later when David wasn't present, I said to Charlie, "My friend, I am going to ask you a question which a number of people are likely to ask you, David and myself if this story ever gets into print. How much liquor had you and David been drinking while you were on that bird hunting trip?"

Now I have known Charlie Blackwood for a good many years and have always found him to be a quiet speaking, very polite individual, but so help me Hannah, I never knew that Charlie possessed a rather sharp temper. But that temper flared when I posed that question about liquor drinking.

"Looka here, man," snapped Charlie, his voice rising to a high crescendo, "we never drank liquor of any kind, rum or beer for at least three days prior to going out on that trip and we certainly never took any out in the boat with us."

"Sorry Charlie," I apologized. Then right on the heels of my apology I risked another outburst from Charlie when I ventured, somewhat timidly, "I suppose those creatures wouldn't have been seals, now would they?"

"Hell, man," exploded Charlie, "have you ever known seals to have arms and legs and big human ears stickin' out from the sides of their heads. Furthermore, you wouldn't see seals climbing a twelve foot cliff. I want you to know that David and I have known every type of seal that was ever pupped from the time we were small boys up to the time we saw those creatures, so we're not so stunned as to mistake them for seals." Then Charlie snorted disgustedly, "Seals indeed, old buddy. Hell ... cripes."

No Bearskin Rug For Me

'Neath Aurora's flame, I made the claim
That I'd shoot me a polar bear,
As I thought 'twould me nice for this king of the ice
To recline by my rocking chair.
And to say to him, when my eyes grew dim,
To my favourite grandchild tot,
Right here by my chair is the polar bear
That your sturdy grandpa shot.

My plans were made and the hunt was splayed
All over the Arctic waste
With my Eskimo Sluk, but we had no luck,
As across the floes we paced.
Now the Eskimo he, oft said to me,
That he was lucky as sin,
But by now I'd despair of getting my bear,
For his luck seemed wearing thin.

Then one bleak day I was on my way
To the village of Tururak.
By old Sol the sun, I carried no gun,
Just a pack of food on my back.
As along I sped, I espied ahead
Four objects out on the ice.
Though the distance was great I could see first rate
And I named them in a trice.

A mortal dread came into my head,
And I felt my insides speared,
As across the snow, first high then low,
Came sounds most awful and weird.
Now you may shrink from a cliff's high brink,
Or quake at a banshee's wail.
But no fear can pierce, nor chill so fierce,
As the wolf howl on your trail.

To the right I went, and with legs near spent,
I reached a hummock tall,
And to grasp its crest I did my best
But failed to make it at all.
Then at my back I could hear the pack
And feel their slavering breath,
While up my spine, like needles fine
Crept the icy fingers of death.

Now I beg you to jeer not at my fear,
For I thought that I'd reached my end.
Sure how could I know that just below,
The Lord had sent me a friend.
From out of a cleft, six feet to my left
Shot a yellow-white bundle of fur
And it moved so slick, though my eyes are quick
It appeared like a ragged blur.

He struck that pack while their jaws hung slack,
And he hurled them twenty feet.
Two fell on their hacks with broken backs,
For his blows were sure and fleet.
With mighty jaws and rending claws,
He tore another in twain,
The remaining one he hugged like fun,
Then ripped him tail to brain.

Now he ambled off with a husky cough,
While I gasped out a thankful prayer,
He'd come in on my side and saved my hide
That blessed long-sought bear.
And now I would well have to tell
To my little grandchild fair,
But no rug will he see, while he sits on my knee
From the skin of a polar bear.

The Frightened Fisherman:
Sam Green

If certain people who have read the story told by Charlie and David Blackwood are skeptical as to the truthfulness of those two men, then I would like to suggest that they read the stories which follow, as by doing so, they may regard the Blackwoods in a more kindly light.

My maternal grandmother was born and raised in Grand Bank. I heard her tell this story on several occasions. She related how a man of that town, a shore fisherman, during the summer months rowed or sailed out to the fishing grounds in his row dory. Of course, he was compelled to use a row dory for in his day the marine motor had not been invented, the time being before the turn of the present century.

Grandmother, who was in her late teens when the incident occurred, told us that a group of men were standing on the bank that overlooks Grand Bank Gut when they observed the fisherman rowing his dory towards land at a very fast rate of speed. He appeared to be digging in his oar washes and leaning back hard with every stroke he took. In fact, his exertions were so great that it caused a high bow wave to pile up on the dory's stem. The men watching his frantic efforts, although they could not see anything in the water near his dory nor for any distance behind it that would give him cause for concern, realized that something must be very much amiss with him.

As he entered the harbour the men hurried down to meet him. He grounded his dory and was so exhausted that he literally tumbled out of her onto the beach. Then he collapsed into unconsciousness. The men picked him up and carried him to his home which was not far from the shore. His wife directed them upstairs where they laid him on his bed. She then sent her elder child for the doctor, who arrived in a few minutes.

The medical man worked over the fisherman for a while and he regained consciousness. The doctor told the man's wife and the others present that the man had evidently seen something which had frightened him and that he was suffering from shock and exhaustion. With the exception of the man's wife, the doctor ordered everyone to leave the room. He then told the woman that he would administer a sleeping pill which would help the man relax and get some sleep which was exactly what he needed.

"These pills will keep him asleep until morning. When he wakes up, neither you nor anyone else must question him until I have had a chance to examine him again."

The doctor arrived early the next morning and the fisherman woke up shortly afterward. The doctor on examining him stated that he found him greatly improved.

"Sam, you must have received a severe fright while your were out fishing yesterday. Do you feel equal to telling you good wife and me all about it?"

"Yes Doctor," replied Sam. "I will tell you and my missus what happened, in fact, I'm satisfied to tell everyone in Grand Bank what I seen, if they should care to listen and I don't care if people believe me or not."

"Well, I was handlinin' at the time. You know, using a single line. I had me hook baited with squid. I was lucky enough to have caught several fine codfish. Then I baited the hook for about the tenth time and lowered it down, almost instantly I hooked on to something and by the heavy tugs on the line I figured I had snagged a giant codfish. So I hauled up as hard as I could with whatever was on the hook puttin' up quite a fight. It finally broke water right close to my dory. 'Twas then I got the biggest fright I ever got in me life, for instead of the big codfish I was expectin' to see I sees a creature that looked like a man. What I mean is, what I could see of 'im from the waist up looked like some kind of man.

"He had eyes, a nose, a mouth and two large ears. He had arms and hands similar to ours. The only thing different I could see, being the fingers, which were webbed. Of course I couldn't see if he had any legs and feet, because the rest of him was underwater. His features on a round head looked like pictures I've seen of apes and monkeys and his face and body was covered with greyish coloured hair. But what give me the real chillin' fright was when the creature started to mumble some kind of gibberish.

"Then he pointed with one of his hands towards the hook in his mouth as if he was motionin' for me to remove it. I could see that the big handline hook had entered his upper lip and its barb was protruding just under his nose. Well, I got hot and cold all over and I had no intention of puttin' my hand anywhere near its mouth, so I drawed me sheath knife and junked off the line close to his face. Then he disappeared under the water and I shipped me oars and headed for home as fast as the Good Lord would let me.

"Doc," continued Sam, "what I caught must have been some kind of manfish and I sure don't want to see his likes again. I can tell you and my missus one thing and that is, I'll never go fishin' anymore."

According to my grandmother, Sam Green never did.

The Frightened Fisherman:
Steve Malloy

During the Hungry Thirties I was on loan from the Newfoundland Constabulary to the Department of Public Health and Welfare, to investigate able-bodied relief conditions in various sections of the country. I say country because at that time Newfoundland was a separate Dominion.

One fall I had occasion to visit a certain settlement in a certain bay, the names of which I do not see the necessity of recording here.

I obtained the names of the relief recipients and the names of others who had applied for the dole, as it was unpopularly known, from the relieving officer. The official was gazing over my shoulder as I ran down the list. Suddenly he pointed to a name: Steve Malloy.

"It's really too bad that that poor man should be receiving able-bodied relief."

"What's so bad about it?" I asked him. "If he really needs it."

"Well, Steve was one of the hardest working fishermen that ever operated out of this harbour. A real man, very proud of his independence. he went out fishing every chance that he could get and I know he steamed to the fishing grounds some days when it was really too stormy for a fisherman to be on the water, but he was eager to catch fish and he most always got it. I'm sure but for what happened a while back, he would still be independent of the dole list.

"You see," continued the relieving officer, "one day about

three years ago, he went out as usual. He owned a fine, large motor dory and on that occasion he took along two tubs of trawl, fully baited, which he intended to set on his favourite grounds. Apparently he did set them because they weren't in his dory when he returned.

"We never did manage to get any details of what he did after he went to sea. But we could figure out his movements pretty correctly. After he set his trawls there is no doubt but that he waited for a while before he started to underrun them. He probably took the time to have a mugup too, as that was what we usually did. I know, because I was a fisherman myself for twenty years before I got this job. Then, whatever it was that give Steve Malloy the big fright must have occurred while he was underrunning his trawl gear, which apparently caused him to let them go in a hurry, for like I said before, they weren't in his dory when he brought her back.

"On that mornin' four or five of us were standing on the government wharf, when we seen Steve's dory coming in the harbour at top speed. Nothin' unusual about that certainly, as most all fishermen come in fast until they neared the shore. Then they'd slow up and finally shut off the engine altogether when they were the appropriate distance from the wharf. But Steve didn't slow up one bit. He kept that engine runnin' at full cock and when he struck the landwash, his dory ran half of her length right upon the beach, you could hear the propeller grinding into the sand. Steve stopped the engine, we all got to him as he jumped out of his dory. His clothes were saturated with sweat and it was rolling off his face in streams. His eyes were real wild lookin' and he seemed on the verge of collapse.

"We helped him up to his house and laid him on the kitchen couch. His wife and children were in tears.

" 'Steve, have you been hurt?' his wife asked anxiously.

" 'No, me dear,' he moaned, 'I haven't been hurt, but I got one terrible fright while I was out fishin' today.'

" 'Whatever could have frightened you that much?' hi wife then asked him.

" 'I'm never going to tell you, nor anyone else for that matter. It was unbelievable and it wouldn't do any of you one bit of good to know what it was. I'll tell you this though, I'll not go to sea again, never again.'

The relieving officer told me that no amount of persuasion by his wife or brothers could get Steve Malloy to describe the object which had caused him to become so terrified.

The following day I interviewed Steve Malloy. He was a good looking man of about forty-five. He was six feet tall, broad shouldered and deep chested. A typical, hardy Newfoundland fisherman and judging by his massive arms and large hands I knew he must be a very powerful man. He was polite and quiet spoken and always answered me with a yes sir or no sir.

I did not broach the subject of that dark, insidious something which had given him such a soul searing fright a few years before, as I did not deem it appropriate to do so. Actually, that incident was none of my business, but I've often wondered since what could have frightened such an experienced and able-bodied fisherman to cause him to abandon his profession that he dearly loved.

Later the relieving officer told me that Malloy had sold off all of his fishing gear and his dory and refused from the day of the sale to ever put a foot into another boat. Other fishermen of the settlement tried unsuccessfully to retrieve Steve's trawls in an effort to ascertain what had happened to their friend. It was rumoured that Malloy did confide in the parish priest as to what he had hauled up on his trawl that day which had frightened him so badly. If he did the reverend gentleman never divulged the secret.

When the Starving Seals Invaded

My grandpa wrung out his soggy mitts,
As he paused outside the door,
Then he walked into the back porch,
And threw them on the floor.
He looked very tired and worn
As he to the table went,
I waited until he ate breakfast,
And then, this question I sent,
"Did you get any fish today, Grandpop?"
"I got neither one at all.
How can you get fish when there's none around
Not a single one, large or small."

"Seals have eaten all cod and haddock,
They have eaten all salmon and hake,
You'd be better off if you set your trap
In the middle of a lake.
They have eaten all herring and caplin,
All the flounder and squid and perch,
You'd do just as well if you set your gear
Across the front of a church.
'Cause the fishery's really got finished
After protestors stopped the hunt,
Now all we can do is make firewood
From each trapskiff, dory and punt."

"Do you know what I fears now, me son?
Seein' fish ain't around no more,
You'll see millions and millions, yes, millions of seals
Climbin' right upon the shore.
For by now they's starved with the hunger,
And that hunger will drive 'em mad,
So the next thing they eats is gonna be us
For, we're all they is to be had."

"But Grandpa," I said, "isn't that farfetched,
To thinks seals will eat us people?"
"No b'y, 'tis not and when they arrives
You'd be wise to climb a church steeple."

"You will have to go high, mighty high
To escape from that hungry herd,
As fer meself, I wish I had wings
To take me aloft like a bird."
Just as Grandpa had finished speaking,
A neighbour rushed in to say,
"The way things looks now it could get bad,
For there's millions of seals in the bay.
I knowed this was goin' to happen,
And so did you, Uncle Ned,
If the seals gets into this settlement,
Then tomorrow we'll all be dead."

It was then I heard some unusual sounds,
Which I never had heard before,
'Twas a mewling chorus with a scuffing noise
That came from the harbour shore.
Then the man slewed around in the doorway
And yelled, "Uncle Ned, get your gun,
For they're comin' ashore and when they lands
It sure won't be very much fun!"
Then Uncle Ned, my grandpa,
Took down his old sealing gun,
Now, turning to me, he ordered,
"Climb upon the roof, me son,"

"And when you reaches the top,
Just throw the ladder down,
Me and the others will hold them off
'Til the women and kids leave town."
From the rooftop I could see right plain,
That the seals had landed now,
And had reached the bank which surrounds the cove,

And were climbing over the brow.
I could see whitecoats, bedlamers, hoods and harps,
And those herds filled the whole wide bay,
I shall never forget the things I saw
From Grandpa's roof that day.

I observed old Mr. Maloney
As he walked across Parson's Brook,
While I watched, two dog hoods seized him
He being the first one they took.
They dragged him over the stream's low bank,
And a bunch of old harps rushed in,
That man was devoured in seconds
I thought 'twas a wonderful sin.
Next I saw old Granny Mason,
Trying to cross the road,
In each hand she held a grocery bag
It was quite a heavy load.
Then, some big seals came and knocked her down
And she disappeared from my view,
That poor, dear soul, never had a chance
They ate her and the groceries too.

Then I saw Mrs. Stella Lasky
Run along with her infant boy,
She slipped on some gravel and fell down flat,
Lost her hold on her pride and joy.
Now her screams must have reached to heaven,
They were that loud and wild,
For a cute, little cuddly whitecoat
Had gobbled up her child.
It was then I saw our men lined up,
Like soldiers on parade,
So tall and strong, so brave and true,
What a noble, grand sight they made.

They fired, reloaded and fired again,
Then reloaded and fired some more.
'Til the waters of brook and harbour
Were reddened by blood and gore,
To the great sob-sister protestors
'Twould viewed as a gruesome sight,
But when human lives were endangered
It gave our men every right
To kill the seals that were killing folks
Though, the killings may look severe
But, if those guys hadn't stopped the hunt,
No starving seals would appear.

Though bloody the harbour and bloody the brook,
For this you can take my word,
That all the blood in those waters
Did not come from that big seal herd.
Folks were bleeding and dying on every hand,
As more seals kept coming ashore,
And I closed my eyes to those horrible scenes
For I just couldn't bear to see more.
Now, the odds against our men were too great,
And I heard myself blubber and sob,
For despite their courage and deadly aim,
They just could not halt that mob.

The Reverend Morgan and Father Burke
Had died in the midst of the strife,
There the Salvation captain breathed his last.
Each had tried to save some life,
I was crying now and crying hard,
For I'd lost many friends out there,
Like young Paddy Kelly and Georgie Coates
And our school teacher, Mr. Haire.
Then, a great big, shiny car drove up,
And two protestors got out,
Above the noise of the guns and the seals
I heard them mightily shout,

"Cease firing, cease firing! You murderous brutes!"
And their words were with anger fraught,
"If you continue this senseless slaughter,
All our good work will go for naught."

They cared not that some men had died,
And women and children beside,
They thought of their wallets only
Being filled by a greenback tide,
Sent by bleeding hearts from across the world,
To aid them in stopping the hunt,
And right now poor, innocent people
Were bearing an awful brunt.
My grandpa went up and spoke to them,
But, I couldn't hear what he said,
Then some dog hoods went and seized all three
And tossed them high overhead.

I saw one protestor gain his feet,
And he screamed aloud to the seals,
"You fools, can't you see we're saving your lives?"
Then he died mouthing terrified squeals.
For 'twas all the same when hunger reigned,
All the same to the harp and the hood,
Be it the flesh of a protestor or fisherman,
They both tasted equally good.
Then one by one our men went down,
Overwhelmed by that slavering mob,
My grief was so great that I blethered out loud,
And once more commenced to sob.

It was then, my grandpa shook me hard,
And yelled, "Come, snap out of it b'y,
You was bleatin' like some poor lost lamb,
And besides that, you'd sob and cry."
Yes, 'twas only a dream and I'm mighty glad
Of the fact, things turned out that way,
But, a horrible thought just entered my mind,
That my dream may come true some day.

Springheel Jack

During late September and through October 1929, people in the western back section of St. John's were treated, if you can call it that, to several visits from a strangely dressed, mysterious character. He made his appearance always on Merrymeeting Road and on the rooftops of houses situated along that street. His outlandish apparel, his uncanny ability, which enabled him to leap from the ground to the roof of a house and back again, coupled with his outbursts of violent laughter; details that had been noticed by several people, did have the effect of raising an aura of fear in the community, fear of the unknown.

At least six people saw him and were prepared to swear, if necessary, that they'd had a clear view of him and heard his loud, sardonic laughter. The first person to see him and report on his presence was a middle-age man who was walking along Merrymeeting Road on his way home from work. The time was 6:30 p.m. The man said he was opposite Cook Street. He did not see any person in the street but himself. Then he heard what sounded to him to be loud, insane-like laughter coming from an overhead direction. Glancing skyward he beheld this strangely dressed figure standing on the roof of a nearby house.

He said that he yelled out to the fellow, asking who he was and what he was doing. The only reply was another burst of laughter. Then the figure slipped down over the opposite side of the roof and disappeared. The man thinking that it was just some young man dressed up in an odd looking rig to have some fun for himself, ran through a lane to the back of the house. He was in time to see the roof topper bounding away across St. George's Field. He was not running as the average person runs, but was speeding along in great leaps, covering at least fifteen feet at a jump. He would bounce high in the air, then go ahead in another long leap, just like he had springs in the heels of his boots.

When the account of this man's experience became spread around, it earned for the mysterious stranger the name, 'Springheel Jack'.

The next person to see the springheeled one was a spry seventy-three year old gentleman. He too, was walking on Merrymeeting Road sometime between six and seven in the evening. He observed, he said, that there were no people moving about.

I will explain here that back in those days the usual supper hour for St. John's residents was between six and seven p.m., that is why, within that time, few if any people were seen abroad.

The old gentleman stated he had reached the intersection of Blatch Avenue when the crazy sounding laugh of Springheel Jack came to him from overhead, which caused him to glance upwards. There he saw standing on the saddle of a house this unusual looking being. Like the first man, the old gentleman thinking that it was some young man dressed up for fun, called out to him to get down from the roof.

"You're gonna kill yourself if you fall."

Jack appeared to get a tremendous kick out of this piece of grandfatherly advice, for he laughed louder and longer than before, ending his merriment with several, long drawn "Ki, yi, yi, yi's." He then disappeared over the opposite side of the rooftop. Like I said, this old gentleman was quite spry for his age, so he ran down the lane between the house Jack was perched on and the house next door. He arrived at the back of the houses to observe the sprightly Jack bounding away in what he described as long rabbit-type jumps, as he crossed St. George's Field and disappeared from the old man's view.

The description given by the two men who had seen Springheel Jack tallied exactly. In each case a streetlight shone on the houses where Jack had been standing which illuminated him quite clearly. He was tall, both men said, a six-footer; on his feet he wore a pair of black knee length boots that had a real shine on them. From boot tops to waist he was wearing light coloured tights. From the waist up his dress appeared to be of a somewhat darker material. On his head was a helmet type cap or hat and he wore a black cape over his shoulders. He possessed long, thin features and his pale complexion seemed to have a greenish hue. If Jack was carrying any weapons, he did not attempt to use them on either man.

I was a member of the Newfoundland Constabulary C.I.D. at the time and District Inspector John Byrne, the officer in charge of that department, had received several telephone calls from citizens living in the Merrymeeting Road area, suggesting that they felt it was time for the police to try and capture Springheel Jack and to ascertain his real purpose for being in that area.

As a result of those telephone calls, Inspector Byrne instructed Constable John Walsh and myself to proceed to Merrymeeting Road immediately and to make every effort to catch the bounding Jack and bring him before the inspector for questioning. You could always depend on good old Inspector Byrne to come up with assignments of that nature.

But just before we left the C.I.D. office a report came in which stated that Springheel Jack had been seen by two women a short while before. The guard at the police station who had received the report supplied us with the address of the two women. Walsh and I visited and interviewed them. One of the ladies appeared to be calm and rational, the other one was a nervous wreck.

"Oh, I'll never get over it, I'll never get over it," she moaned. "I only got a brief look at him and that was enough. I'd never believed the stories that were going around about that monster, so when I actually saw him on that rooftop, it was too much."

Her level headed companion who was her sister said, "That's right, one look was all she got and one look was all that I got, for poor Shirley here, fainted dead away and I was so busy trying to attend to her and bring her to, that I didn't have time to worry about Springheel Jack. Although while I was working over Shirley I could hear him laughing and chuckling as if he was making a great joke of my poor sister lying there on the ground. However, when I did get the chance to look up again he had disappeared."

Those two women had been walking along Merrymeeting Road, the time was again between the hours of six and seven p.m., when their attention had been attracted by Jack's wild laughter coming to them from a nearby rooftop. The sighting reported by the two women, coupled with the reports of the two men created quite a stir of indignation and concern in that area of town. Mothers made sure that their children were safely indoors long before dark and no woman would think of venturing on the street after nightfall without a male escort.

At the office of Inspector General Hutchings, at the C.I.D. and at the police station calls were coming in demanding full police protection from this character. Rumours began circulating to the effect that Springheel Jack was an escaped mental patient. No inmate had been reported as missing from the local institution, but when that fact was pointed out, certain people had answers for that too. He had escaped from some lunatic asylum up in Canada or in the United States, and was just awaiting a favourable opportunity to pounce on some luckless individual and slash his throat. As can be seen, up to that time, Jack had had the opportunity to attack two men and two women, yet he hadn't pounced.

The demand for police protection from the public brought results. Back in those days, the constabulary could only muster some thirty-five men for active duty and five of those were members of the C.I.D. The district inspector in charge of street duties was instructed to detail two uniformed constables to patrol Merrymeeting Road along the fronts of the houses. One was to cover the area between Newtown Road and Mayor avenue, the other from Mayor avenue to Freshwater Road. He also detailed two constables, dressed in plain clothes, to patrol along by the backyards of the Merrymeeting Road houses. In addition, Constable Walsh and I were instructed to cover the area whenever possible.

In the meantime, a group of men and teenage boys formed themselves into a vigilante group. They were armed with fence pickets and baseball bats and they swore vengeance on Springheel Jack if they ever caught up with him. Well, they didn't catch Springheel Jack, but they did catch one of the plain clothes policemen who was patrolling along by the backyards, namely, Constable Gus Pike. Although Constable Pike in no way resembled the description which had been given of the jumping Jack, the mob seized him roughly and accused him of being that individual. In vain Pike tried to inform them that he was a plain clothes policeman. Then one of the ringleaders shouted for him to show his badge. Pike reached into his pocket for the badge, then to his dismay, remembered that he had left it on the dining room table at home. The crowd would have undoubtedly given Pike a rough going over, if one of the uniformed policemen hadn't arrived on the scene and rescued him. On receiving Pike's report of the incident, Inspector General Hutchings posted notices ordering the vigilantes to disband or else...they disbanded.

John Walsh and I had just reported back to the C.I.D. office one evening when the telephone rang; Walsh answered it. The lady on the other end of the line told him, that if a policeman was sent round to her house she could give him a good report on the scoundrel that people called Springheel Jack. She gave a Merrymeeting Road address. Telling the woman that we would get there as soon as possible, Walsh broke the connection.

I would like to insert here that in those days the police, including the NCO's of the C.I.D. and the street patrol, did not enjoy the luxury of patrolling around in government issue cars, for the very good reason that no cars were supplied to them. One car only was issued and paid for with tax dollars and that was the vehicle which was driven by Inspector General Hutchings or his chauffeur, and was intended exclusively for his use. Even the second in command of the force, Superintendent P.J. O'Neill, was not supplied with a government car.

In view of the foregoing, Constable Walsh and I were, of course, obliged to walk from the police station where the C.I.D. office was housed, overlooking Water Street to Merrymeeting Road. We duly arrived at the lady's residence, which was situated near the western end of that street.

She was a short, sturdily built person, who I would judge to be around forty years of age. She told us that she had been down in the east end visiting relatives and was walking along Merrymeeting Road on her way home. The time was around seven p.m. When she reached the intersection of Mayor Avenue, she was alerted by a series of loud chuckles coming from overhead.

"I looked upward," she continued, "and there standing on the edge of a roof, on the east side of Mayor Avenue, was none other than his honour, Mr. Springheel Jack. I can tell you gentlemen right now," she said, "he didn't cause me any fright, on the contrary, the very sight of that brazen character made me see red, I got really mad. So I yelled to him, 'How dare you to be going around in that fancy rigout scaring women and poor little children half to death? Just you come down here, you rascal, and I'll beat your head off with my handbag.'"

But the springheeled one declined to accept the challenge offered to him by the courageous little woman. For he stayed where he was and started to laugh uproariously, as if he were highly amused at the idea of a woman being prepared to engage him in combat.

"Now gentlemen," she continued, "I know that you are not going to believe this and I don't expect you to, but you can take me before any judge or magistrate in this city and I will willingly and honestly swear to what I saw Jack do next. Well, he spread his cape and actually flew right across Mayor Avenue, then landed on a housetop on the opposite side. Do you know?" she asked, "When he landed on that roof, he had the gall to wave to me, then he let go with another crazy laugh and disappeared over the back side of the house."

There you have it. Was that little lady telling the truth? She certainly appeared to be a very sincere person and apart from seeming somewhat irate while she was telling us of her experience, she showed no signs of nervousness or fear. Although the image of Springheel Jack becoming airborne does look to be rather incredulous.

Despite the fact that uniformed and plain clothes police patrols never let up after Jack had appeared in view of the woman who had fainted dead away at the sight of him, only one policeman ever saw the lively jumper and got close to him. That was Constable Guy Porter, a six foot, two inch, one hundred and ninety pound, former lumberjack. Porter was alone on patrol on Merrymeeting Road, his partner having been withdrawn to other duty. His beat extended from Newtown Road to Mayor Avenue. At around 6:30 p.m. that evening the constable was approaching Mayor Avenue when he heard a loud burst of laughter issuing from an overhead direction. Looking heavenward, the officer beheld the character, which had been so adequately described by others who had seen him. He was standing upright on the roof of a house that was and probably still is, situated on the corner of Merrymeeting Road and Mayor Avenue. In fact he was on the same dwelling where the lady who had offered to soften his head with her handbag had reported seeing him. The constable called out to him, telling him he was under arrest and to get down immediately. Did Springheel Jack obey that official summons? Not he. He did not speak a word, but he waved gaily to the policeman and laughed loud and long. Then he bounced across two more rooftops and disappeared from Porter's view over the backyard side of the houses. The officer threw off his belt and discarded his heavy greatcoat, then ran down Mayor Avenue until he reached the backs of the houses. Expecting to see Jack disappearing in the distance, he was greatly surprised to see him standing still, about sixty feet away. It was quite obvious to Porter that laughing boy had actually waited for him to show up. As the constable approached the still figure, he again advised him that he was under arrest. Jack's reply was another hearty laugh. Then he wheeled about and bounded away in long leaps. Porter gave chase, ordering Jack to halt, but the only response the officer got was another wild burst of laughter.

The pursuit crossed St. George's field, crossed Newtown Road, and reached the fence surrounding Shamrock Field. At that time it was a wooden fence at least six feet in height. Springheel Jack cleared it in a single bound, straight up and over; Porter, with a bit of a scramble cleared the fence also. But when he struck the ground on the opposite side of the fence, he knew he was out of the race, for in landing he had badly sprained his left ankle. He could only sit on the ground and groan while Jack bounded off and disappeared into the darkness. Limping badly, Porter made his way to the Central Fire Hall, where he telephoned a report of the incident to District Inspector Stephen Noseworthy, the officer in charge of the police station.

The inspector mustered all the men he could locate, which included the five of us from the C.I.D. and a thorough search was made over the whole Merrymeeting Road area, but we did not succeed in catching the slippery Springheel Jack. He had vanished completely, and as far as I am aware, from that day to this (1986), that unusually dressed, agile, loud-laughing character was never seen again.

It was apparent that when he stood still long enough for Constable Porter to approach him closely, then bound away and easily keep ahead of his pursuer, he was, in the opinion of many, displaying his utter contempt in the ability of the husky policeman to overtake and capture him. It was obvious also, that he desired to make his final exit from the scene with a grandiose exhibition of his prowess.

Although Springheel Jack did create an atmosphere of dread when he was making those rooftop appearances, he never committed any acts of violence, nor was it ever reported that he had entered or attempted to enter any of the dwellings in the area. Whatever sort of ingenious device he had fastened in or on his boots that enabled him to make those long, high leaps is still a secret. Two of the houses on which he was seen were not equipped with ladders. How did he manage to get upon those roofs and down again so quickly, without that aid? Could he have gained the roofs of those two story houses, the saddles of which were at least thirty feet from the ground, then return to terra firma with a single bound? One would imagine this to be an impossible feat without him suffering injury or death as a result.

Over in England, many years ago, an individual wearing apparel which was very similar to that worn by the local Jack and who matched him in height and build was capable of doing that and laughing loudly while he was performing the stunt. That being was first seen in 1837 by some people who were crossing a common in southwest London. They reported seeing an alarming figure passing by them flying in great leaps through the air. Apparently other citizens paid little attention to the report. Then a year later, in 1838, a young woman was attacked by this character. He tore her dress, he pinned her head under his arm and clawed her body. Her sister on hearing her screams, ran out and called for help. But before anyone could stop him, he bounded away and disappeared. Later, the girl, when describing her attacker to police officers, said he was wearing a kind of helmet and a tight fitting costume. His face, she told them was hideous, his eyes were like balls of fire, his hands had great claws and he vomited blue and white flames.

Sometime later, an eighteen year old girl, named Lucy Scales, was on her way home one evening with her sister, when suddenly a tall, cloaked figure leaped out of the shadows and spat blue flames in Lucy's face, blinding her.

Our people named the local, laughing jumper Springheel Jack, over in England they added an *ed* to that name, over there he was called Spring-heeled Jack.

During the 1850s and 1860s, Spring-heeled Jack was sighted all over England. In the 1870s army authorities set traps for him, after sentries reported being frightened by a man who leaped out of the darkness to slap their faces with an ice cold hand, then spring upon the roofs of their sentry boxes. But the army didn't succeed in catching him.

The description of countless witnesses concerning his appearances were always the same; the long, high leaps, the raucous laughter, the hellish, glowing eyes and the blue flames were reported. On one occasion some angry men fired their guns at him, whether any of the bullets struck him nobody can say, but apparently he suffered no injury, for he laughed loudly at the shooters' efforts and promptly disappeared.

Spring-heeled Jack's glowing eyes were seen in Liverpool in 1904, sixty-seven years after the first sightings. There, he put on quite a show, causing panic. He kept bounding up and down the streets, leaping from the cobblestones to the rooftops and back again. When a few courageous men attempted to corner him, he laughed and vanished in the darkness from whence he came. It was his final appearance.

Back in 1929, in St. John's, a question was asked, the same question that was asked over in England several years before. Who or what was Springheel Jack? That question was never answered. I presume that if the leaping Jacks turn up in this modern time of flying saucers, certain persons would proclaim that they were aliens from a space ship.

I feel that I should make one more reference to the English character. When he was first observed in 1837, he was described as being tall and seemed to be fully developed. So suggesting that he was twenty years old at that time and assuming that he was the same person who had made appearances all over England for sixty-seven years, he would have been eighty-seven years old when he put on his great cobblestones to rooftops show in 1904. Once again, if he were that same individual who possessed the ability to perform so nimbly at nearly ninety years of age then I for one would sure like to learn the secrets of his keep-fit and acrobatic agility.

Dot Crow

It was on April 22, 1923, that I strolled east on Water Street and walked out on the Furness Withy pier. A steamer, the *Canadian Sapper,* was tied up there discharging cargo. I observed an officer standing on deck smoking a cigar. I approached him and asked if the ship needed any crewmen. He invited me to come aboard. He told me that he was the chief steward and that his name was Kelly. Then in reply to my question, he advised me that he required a steward for the officer's mess. He asked if I'd ever served on a ship as a steward and I told him no. He looked me up and down for a moment or two.

"You can have the job if you want it. But," he added, "if you do not perform your duties in a manner that's suitable to me on your first trip to Montreal, when we return here in two weeks or so, ashore you go."

I told Mr. Kelly that I would very much like to have the job and assured him that I would certainly do my best to prove I could handle it.

"Alright then, report to me here at nine o'clock tomorrow morning and bring your gear along."

I thanked him and left. I arrived back on the Furness Withy pier at a quarter to nine the following morning, April 23, St. George's Day, to discover the *Canadian Sapper* gone. A group of longshoremen were standing on the pier head and I enquired of them if they knew the whereabouts of the steamer. One of them replied that she had been moved up to the west end of the harbour late the evening before. I thought it possible that Mr. Kelly had not known of the impending move as he had made no mention of it to me.

I had with me a fairly large suitcase, crammed with all my possessions. So I trudged west on Water Street with that miserable suitcase becoming heavier and heavier and more obnoxious as I proceeded. I located the *Sapper* as far up in the

west end of the harbour as she could get without actually
going on drydock. I went aboard and one of the deckhands
pointed out the chief steward's cabin to me.

I knocked on the door and Mr. Kelly yelled for me to go
in. After I'd entered, he explained that the ship's company
was very upset.

"Our second engineer, Ashton Jolliffe is missing. After
we'd moved the ship up here last evening, Jolliffe was seen
entering his cabin and everybody was under the impression
that he'd eventually gone ashore. Captain James Jolliffe had
come on board earlier seeking his son," Kelly said. "They live
here in town and Ashton's mother is very ill and it certainly
isn't like him not to visit her while he's in port."

At Captain Jolliffe's request, he had gone to Ashton
Jolliffe's cabin but he wasn't there; then he had made enquir-
ies all over the ship, but no one had seen the second engineer
since the evening before. As Mr. Kelly's search had proven
fruitless, Captain Jolliffe left the *Sapper* to report his son's
disappearance to the police.

Shortly after my arrival on board, two police constables
arrived in a dory and with cod jiggers commenced to drag the
waters of the harbour near the ship. They kept trying without
success until 2 p.m. when the ship was moved once more, this
time over to the Imperial Oil Company's wharf on the south
side. We had been at that location only half an hour when our
captain was notified that the two policemen had recovered
the second engineer's body.

In the meantime, the chief steward had taken me along
to the officer's messroom which was situated in the after
section of the ship's superstructure. When we entered the
room I noticed a grey haired man, who appeared to be about
sixty years old, seated there drinking coffee. Mr. Kelly intro-
duced him to me as Mr. Angel, the chief engineer. I later
discovered that Mr. Angel was a Welshman and that he always
pronounced the word *that* as *dot*.

The chief steward outlined my duties. First he informed me that the officers who would be occupying the messroom during meal hours were: the chief, second and third officers; the chief, second and third engineers; the wireless operator and himself. The table was littered with dirty dishes.

Mr. Kelly instructed, "First you will wash and dry those dirty dishes and stow them, neatly, away in their racks on the wall. You will serve the officers their meals on time and piping hot. You must also sweep and mop the floor regularly and polish all the brass work, you have to see to it that this room is kept generally tidy."

He then took me to the galley and introduced me to the cook, who was diminutive, but he appeared to be a cocky individual whose name was Keeping, which he himself pronounced as Kippin. He was a Newfoundlander. He told me later he'd been born on Burnt Islands near Rose Blanche, but had run away to sea when he was only twelve years old and had followed the sea ever since; he was then thirty-five.

My other duties included helping the cook by peeling and washing the vegetables he would need during the day. Off the galley was the cook's cabin, which contained two bunks, the upper I found was mine. I returned to the officer's mess to tackle the dish-washing chore. Before I got the chance to begin, Mr. Angel came in and sat down. He asked me to go to the galley and fetch him a cup of coffee. When I'd placed it before him, he stared gloomily into the brew for a while.

"I knew something like dot would happen."

"Something like what, sir?" I enquired.

"Like the second engineer getting drowned," he replied. "Do you know boy, dot on our way down here from Montreal, a crow come on board this ship and strutted around on the after deck as if he owned her. Yes, a crow, mind you. You know boy, a crow is a bird of the land, whereas it is true dot they sometimes fly over salt water, they only go a few yards off shore, but at the time dot creature boarded us, we were fully fifteen miles at sea.

"You see," continued the chief engineer, "the crow is a bird of ill omen and over in the old country, no person in his right senses will permit one to alight on his house or any other building come to that, if he can help it. So when dot crow landed on the deck of the *Sapper*, I was sure some member of our crew was going to become the victim of an accident and I was right," he finished.

Shortly afterward, Mr. Angel went ashore to hunt for another second engineer. He returned at 6 p.m. with a stocky, bowlegged Scotsman by the name of Ian MacCafferty, who looked to be in his thirties. He held a second engineer's ticket. Mr. MacCafferty had been highly recommended to Mr. Angel by the ship's agents as a very capable man.

At six o'clock the following morning, two fishermen from the Battery came alongside with a half boat load of salmon. Amongst the catch was one exceptionally large fish. It measured three feet in length and weighed fifty-five pounds. It was a perfect specimen. Mr. Angel bought it.

Which brings to mind the great differences in salmon catches in 1923 compared to what they are today. The fishermen's boat was an eighteen footer and she was half loaded from a single morning's haul. I presume that if you hauled all the salmon nets right up the Southern Shore today, you'd hardly get that many fish.

The cook also purchased a number of salmon for the ship's use and the fishermen went on their way. The chief engineer handed his salmon over to me and told me to take it down to the lazarette and place it in the ice box.

"You look after dot salmon, like a good boy and keep it covered with ice all the time. When we get to Montreal, I will have it stuffed and mounted and give it to my sister for a birthday present."

At 7 a.m., we steamed out of St. John's Harbour, bound

for Montreal. The trip along the south coast of Newfound-
land went very well. There were no wind storms, heavy seas
or fog to hamper us. The old *Sapper* ploughed her way along
while I served meals, washed dishes, mopped floors, polished
brass and peeled spuds. We eventually passed out of sight of
the Newfoundland coast and headed for the coast of Gaspé.

We steamed along for an hour or so, breakfast had been
served, the dirty dishes washed and stowed away. The cook
and I, along with a young seaman named Paddy Sparrow
were standing on deck aft of the main superstructure; sud-
denly, Sparrow, who was gazing out over the starboard quar-
ter yelled.

"Be the hook, block and iron pin, here comes that crow
again."

Other crew members who'd heard Sparrow's an-
nouncement took up the cry.

"The crow, the crow!" was heard on all sides. Mr. Angel
appeared as if by magic, one would suspect that he was just
standing by as if he were expecting a return of the black
feathered visitor. The bird circled around the stern of the
ship, then alighted on the centre of the after hatch cover. Mr.
Angel screamed to us to drive dot creature away. No one
moved, we were enjoying the antics of the crow, who was
strutting about with the same air of independence and com-
mand that the captain exhibited when he walked the bridge.
The chief engineer seized a deck broom which was leaning
against the rail and took off after the crow. He nearly met
disaster right away for he tripped in a length of rope that was
stretched across the deck and fell flat on his face, but he
quickly got to his feet and made a wild swipe with his broom.
It was a complete miss, for the black bird had hopped nimbly
to one side as the weapon descended. Mr. Angel tried again,
yelling meanwhile for the crow to get off the ship, but once
more the crow eluded him. Then the chief made a third try,
but apparently the bird decided to take no further chances,

he spread his wings, flew up over the rail and took off. He soon disappeared in the distance.

While Mr. Angel had been making violent, but futile attempts to clobber the crow, we'd all been laughing uproariously at his efforts. Now the mussed up and sweaty chief came up to us and wagged his finger in our faces.

"You may laugh," he told us sternly, "but mark my words, there'll be another accident aboard here before very long." Then he left the deck.

"Poor, foolish, superstitious old man," chuckled the cook. "I know now, that harmless crow landin' on our deck has a lot to do with accidents."

But those words were scarcely out of the cook's mouth when a loud cry came from the direction of the engine room.

"Man killed!" shouted the voice.

We all rushed to the doorway leading to the engine room and beheld Mr. Riley, the third engineer who with the donkeyman, Mike O'Brian, was toiling up the ladder bearing a limp form between them. They brought the man out and laid him down on deck. I knew him only as Peter, he was one of the firemen. Peter had a large bump on his forehead. We had no ship's doctor, but the wireless operator, who was a first aid man, did any patching up that was necessary. The fireman was not dead, but he was unconscious, probably as a result of that blow to the head. The wireless operator and the captain arrived together with the crow-hating Mr. Angel right behind them. The wireless man told Riley and O'Brian to bring the injured man into his cabin and lay him on the bunk.

Now the old chief turned to us, rather triumphantly, I thought, and said, "Ah ha, I see you fellows are not laughing now. I told you before and I'm telling you again, dot crow is an evil bird and every time he boards us an accident will happen to some member of our crew."

The wireless operator's examination of Peter disclosed

that in addition to the head bump, he'd suffered a badly sprained right wrist and a broken right collar bone. Of course, there was no way for the wireless man to tell if he had sustained any internal injuries. When we reached Quebec City, Captain Bluin had him taken ashore to hospital; we left him there.

When the fireman regained consciousness, he said he met with the accident while he was walking along on the top deck. Somebody had removed the grating which covered the opening leading to the coal bunker. As Peter walked, he was gazing seaward and did not notice the hole. He stepped right into it and fell a distance of fifteen feet, down on top of the pile of coal.

We finally docked at Montreal. It was Paddy Sparrow's and also my first visit to that big city. So after supper was cleared away we got ready to go ashore. As we were about to leave, Mr. Angel arrived in a raging temper.

"Where is dot salmon I gave you to look after?" he shouted at me.

I told him I saw it in the ice box just before we docked.

"Well, it's not there now," he yelled. "Someone has stolen it and I'm holding you responsible for not guarding it properly."

"Don't be ridiculous Chief," I told him. "It was not a part of my duty to stand guard on your salmon the whole twenty-four hours of every day and you're certainly not holding me responsible for its disappearance."

Still furious, Mr. Angel turned about, quickly walked up the gangplank and stepped ashore.

Paddy and I walked around the city seeing the sights. We came back aboard just before dark, as we had been advised the waterfront of Montreal was an unhealthy place to be after nightfall. I climbed into my bunk and promptly fell asleep.

The Canadian Merchant Marine, who owned the *Sapper* and over a half hundred ships, had its own police force. Two uniformed constables were on duty in the freight shed adjoining the pier day and night. During the daylight hours there was a sergeant present as well. Those officers kept an eagle eye trained on seamen passing along from ship to shore and vice versa. Their surveillance was most particularly directed to seamen on their way back to the steamers, for members of ship's companies had been known to steal items from the shed and smuggle them aboard. Those policemen, I'd notice, appeared to be vigilant and I was sure that it would be most difficult for any seaman who decided to steal some article from the shed and bring it aboard to escape undetected.

There was also a strict order posted by the management to the effect that no man serving on any of their ships was permitted to bring aboard beer or liquor. Of course, the beer or liquor smugglers would be in exactly the same position as the thief, they would be forced to elude the two officers on shed duty.

At that time the province of Quebec was wet, you could buy all the beer or liquor you may require there. I understood too, at the same time all other provinces of Canada with the exception of British Columbia were dry, because prohibition reigned.

I was rudely awakened by somebody shaking my shoulder. I gazed up into the slitted eyes of the cook. He was loaded to the gills. I saw by my old turnip * hanging on the wall, that it was twenty minutes after midnight. The cook informed me that he was going to become a very rich man, then he elaborated.

"You know, Charlottetown, P.E.I is bone dry on account of this prohibition horse apples, which as it happens is real good for me. I have just brought aboard four brin bags full of Molson's Ale. I paid twenty cents a bottle for it, but when we

---

* A colloquial term for pocket watch.

get to Charlottetown, we always stop there on the way down,
I'll sell my ale for a dollar fifty a bottle." Here the cook winked
and thumped me on the chest.

"Of course," he said, "I had to pay a taxi driver one dollar
to carry it from the tavern and that miserable tavern keeper
charged me fifty cents for the four bags but those amounts are
only chicken feed. So kid, you can see by me plan, in a few
trips I'll be pretty wealthy."

"But Cook," I asked him, "how did you manage to smug-
gle all that beer aboard with those two policemen on guard
out there?"

"I'll tell you a little secret, because I trusts you not to
squeal on me. You may not be aware of it kid, but you are
shipmates with one of the smartest men who ever crossed the
Gulf of St. Lawrence, namely me." He winked again and I got
another thump on the chest. "The secret is, I gave the police
sergeant old Angel's big salmon and he told his two men that
if they saw me bringing any packages aboard to look the other
way. As you knows, I'm a very small man and not too strong,
so when I looked over those two big, strappin' policemen in
the shed, the thought struck me that those guys were in better
shape to lug that beer aboard than me. So I sneaked down to
the lazarette and picked up two more salmon I'd bought in St.
John's and gave the policemen one each. Now, those salmon
while not near the old Chief's in size, were fine, sturdy fish all
the same and the boys were mighty glad to get 'em. After that,
they shouldered my beer and brought it to the galley for me."

The cook then took me out to the galley and showed me
his precious Molson's Ale, after which I went back to my bunk.
Drunk and all as he was, Keeping managed to stow it out of
sight, in various nooks and crannies of our cabin, the galley
and the storeroom that led off it, every bottle of ale. Then he
remained spry and alert enough to cook breakfast after-
wards.

We remained in Montreal for two days, then we steamed

out and headed for Charlottetown. We were delayed at the
Island's capital for only a day discharging cargo. The cook
managed to sell a lot of his Molson's to longshoremen
working on the ship. Many of them got too drunk to work
which caused no end of confusion. We left for St. John's the
next morning.

When we reached a certain latitude, that several crew
members swore was the exact location of his previous visits,
the black bird boarded us again. The crow was heard all over
the ship and Mr. Angel raced from his cabin. The crow had
again landed on the after hatch cover. Mr. Angel turned to a
couple of sailors standing near and shouted for them to get
rid of dot evil bird. The feathered one did not appear to be
one bit disturbed by the chief's shouting, for he strutted about
as calmly as before. Anyway, the two seamen went after him,
but as they came near, he spread his wings, emitted several
raucous caw caws and flew away.

The chief engineer became very upset, "We will have
another accident very soon," he predicted.

And do you know, the old man was right, for the crow had
no sooner disappeared from view when someone roared,
"Man killed!"

That unwelcome announcement sounded as if it had
come from the port side. Several of us rushed over there and
discovered a middle-aged seaman named Tommy Newport
lying face down on deck with a heavy ash chute resting across
his neck. One of the firemen was trying to lift it off him; with
the help of two other men, the piece of equipment was
removed. Newport was not dead, but he was out cold and had
suffered a nasty cut on the back of his neck, which was
bleeding profusely. The men lifted him up and carried him
to the wireless operator, where Sparks, as he was more
familiarly known, rendered first aid.

The ash chute was made of heavy sheet iron with a double
edged rim and it must have weighed nearly one hundred

pounds. It had been manufactured with a strong curve, so that when it was positioned overside, the outer end was pointed downward towards the sea, while the curve allowed the inboard end or mouth to remain upright, permitting articles dumped into it free access to the water. All ashes from the stokehold, as well as ashes and garbage from the galley were deposited overboard via this chute.

It appears that Newport had received orders from Mr. Guthreau, the third officer, to pull in the chute and give it a coat of paint. After he'd pulled it in Tommy had jammed it up against the ladder leading to the bridge, in what he considered was a safe position. Then he started painting. There was a bit of a swell in the water at the time and the *Sapper* was taking it on the broadside which caused her to roll a little. One extra heavy swell came along and the ship rolled a little further over than usual, with the result that the chute broke free from the ladder and started to topple down. Newport saw it falling and made an attempt to step aside to avoid it when he slipped and fell heavily face down on deck and the chute crashed down on the back of his neck.

The fact that the chute was curved saved Tommy Newport's life. For as it fell, the man's neck fitted rather loosely underneath that curve. It connected with him enough to inflict the cut, but caused no serious injury. Had the chute landed three inches to the right or the left, Newport's head would have been severed from his body. He was evidently knocked out when his head struck the hard, steel deck as he fell.

After Newport's accident, Mr. Angel's beliefs and prophecies regarding the crow were no longer being ridiculed. In fact, all hands were now treating him with the greatest respect.

I never did learn if the crow again visited the *Canadian Sapper* after that one and only trip I made on her. For as we were entering the Narrows of St. John's Harbour, Mr.

Pheaney, the second steward, came along and roughly or-
dered me to perform a duty which was his to do. I refused and
he called me a bastard. I punched him square in the mouth,
knocking him down and splitting both lips while his blood
started to flow freely. The harbour pilot now had charge of
the ship and she was nearing the Furness Withy pier. Captain
Bluin appeared on the scene. Pheaney showed him his cut
lips and accused me of assaulting him without provocation.
In vain I tried to explain to the captain that Pheaney started
it all and he'd called me a bastard, but Captain Bluin refused
to listen to me and took sides with the second steward.

"You are fired," he snarled. "Just as soon as we are
docked, pack your dunnage and go."

As I was getting my things together, the cook came into
our cabin. He was bleary-eyed and reeked of stale Molson's
and sour underwear. He was still under the influence, which
caused me to suspect that he'd retained a few bottles of the ale
for his own use, to guzzle on the way down.

The cook shook my hand, "I'm sorry to see you go kid, but
in another way I'm glad for your own sake that you're leavin',
for this packet is fast becomin' a hell ship." Then he winked
an eye, dug a thumb in my mid-section and cautioned me,
"Don't mention this to a soul, but a few minutes ago I seen
three rats leave the ship, so you know what's goin' to happen
to her? Well, I'll tell you. She's gonna be lost, with all hands,
that's what. For when rats leave a ship, she'll go down b'y."

"But Cook, if that happens won't you go down with the
ship?"

"Not me kid," he replied. "I'm one of the smart ones, I
knows how to take care of meself."

There was one thing I was pretty sure of, if the cook
continued swilling that ale, he'd probably be seeing rats all
over the place before midnight.

Captain Bluin was standing on the gangplank when I
reached deck. He headed for the shipping office and I

followed along, no word was spoken. I went through the formalities of signing off the *Sapper's* crew list and was given my discharge papers and what money I had coming to me. I then walked over to Harvey's number one pier where the S.S. *Sable Island* was berthed.

I asked a sailor swabbing down the deck if the ship needed any crewmen and he pointed to a door labelled Chief Officer. I knocked on the door. It was opened by a short, stocky, red-faced man with three gold rings on his sleeves.

I said, "Do you need any men, sir?"

"Men we need, not boys." Then he smiled, "Can you steer?"

"Yes sir."

"Then go and stow your gear in the spare bunk in the fo'c'sle. I will sign you on later, we'll be leaving in less than an hour, so be ready to go to work the moment we are off from the wharf."

I was more than delighted to secure a berth on the *Sable Island* only half an hour after being fired off the *Canadian Sapper*. The chief officer was Michael Kane, he hailed from Antigonish, Nova Scotia. Joining the crew of the *Sable Island* meant also that I was elevated from the position of messroom steward to that of able seaman.

To return to the *Canadian Sapper*, with regard to Mr. Angels' superstitious beliefs concerning the arrival of the black bird and the accidents that followed his visits. It can be argued that these were simply a series of coincidences. But when you come to size it up, what the heck was a traditionally land-hugging creature like dot crow doing fifteen miles at sea anyway?

My Life Was Saved By...?

One afternoon I was hunting birds
Out on a wintry bight,
When clouds rolled up like dirty curds
And snowflakes came in sight,
In less time than it takes to tell
The storm came rushing down,
It blotted out the harbour bell,
Then blotted out the town.

And then although 'twas winter time,
Strong lightning flashed out bright,
While thunder rolled its deafening rhyme
And the day turned dark as night,
The wind was raging in its might,
I felt I'd breathe no more,
While stinging blasts had dimmed my sight,
With cold my lungs were sore.

Broadside, my dory struck a rock,
Which dumped me in the brine,
Soon I was stung by icy shock
That stabbed with barb and tine,
The water did not reach my chin,
But my legs were rubber slack,
And every wave that threw me in
Their retreat just dragged me back.

I knew I could not last too long
In that cold winter sea,
And then my heart burst out in song
When a voice spoke close to me,
By mighty hands my wrists were grasped
And I was pulled to land,
With strength near spent my thanks I gasped,
Then sank down on the sand.

And then the lightning flashed again,
While by its lurid glow
I saw my rescuer quite plain,
Whose beard was white as snow,
A little man all bent and lame
I'd never seen before,
Although I thought that I could name
Each man on our shore.

Now I weigh fourteen stone or more,
And six foot one's my height,
While this little man stood five foot four
And in pounds weighed very light.
I figured I was seeing wrong,
With my head shocked by the storm,
For how could that man be so strong
Yet old and frail of form.

And then he led me up the beach,
'Til we gained my father's place,
I had the door within my reach
When he vanished without a trace,
I told my dad about my plight,
And the man who'd pulled me in,
His face took on a look of fright,
And he turned as white as gin.

Now after I had told my tale,
My father grasped a book,
Then opened up its pages stale,
And bade me take a look,
That picture there! I gasped, amazed,
It's the man who saved my life,
My parent still appeared quite dazed,
Then his words pierced like a knife.
Said he, "My son, to be here now
You are luckier than most,
But I'm prepared to swear and vow,
You were saved by Grandpa's ghost."

Haunted Men: George Castle

As the characters in the following accounts had arrived, tarried for awhile and took their departure before I was born, I never had the privilege of meeting them. Nor did they return in our area again.

Apparently those men were wanderers, or as such types were called during the old days in the western United States, drifters. That is to say they never seemed to be able to settle down permanently. The place where three of those men resided for a brief period was in my old hometown of Lamaline, Newfoundland.

My maternal grandfather was awakened one night around the middle of October 1880, by a pain in his upper right arm. This pain was not too severe at first but as time went on it grew progressively worse. He was a fisherman. By the end of January 1881, even if the fishing operations had been in progress he would have been unable to work a codjigger or handline or set and haul a codnet or a trawl.

The doctor at Grand Bank could not diagnose the cause of his illness, but he did give him some pills to take which would deaden the pain and permit him to get some sleep.

Just after my grandfather had first become ill, around the tenth of November, a knock came on the back door. In those days when somebody knocked on your door, you knew that it had to be a stranger, for no neighbour or friend bothered to knock on doors, they just opened them and walked in. My grandmother answered the knock, a man was standing there, a total stranger. He appeared to be a man around sixty years or so. He was six feet tall and of a slim build. He told her that

70

he had walked all the way from Grand Bank, a distance of twenty-eight miles. He was polite and well spoken. He was an Englishman he told her and that he had left his home some forty years before and had not since returned.

He continued, "I would be greatly obliged if you could put me up for the winter. I'm quite prepared to do any kind of work that's required."

He did not seek wages, all he would need was his food and a place to sleep. He appeared to be sincere in all his statements and my grandmother was impressed with his manner generally, so she invited him in and introduced him to my ailing grandfather. He said his name was George Castle.

The people who lived in the west end of the harbour of Lamaline suffered one severe handicap, that was the lack of drinking water. The spit of land on which the houses were built was more commonly known as the meadow. At some time in the distant past this piece of land had evidently been made by the sea, for underneath the sod in most places you would find sand and beach gravel. From time to time wells had been dug there but the water was too salty to drink. This was not too surprising seeing that the ocean lay to the south, the harbour to the east and a mile long barachois lay to the north and west. So during the summer months water had to be dipped up in barrels from a sweetwater spring that never ran dry. The spring was situated above the upper end of the barachois, and the barrels placed in dories for transportation. During the winter months it had to be hauled by horse or ox from a pond that lay one mile west of the settlement. It stood to reason that if my grandfather would have been unable to handle fishing gear he would be likewise unable to cut firewood or freight down drinking water. Everyone at that time heated their homes with wood. It was very necessary for the menfolk to cut down a supply of wood in the fall of sufficient quantity to last throughout the winter.

My grandfather took a liking to George Castle on sight

and he agreed to take him on according to the terms Mr. Castle had suggested. Actually I suspect he considered that the old Englishman had arrived in the nick of time for he needed help badly.

The next morning, Castle proved that he was a worker alright, for at my grandmother's request, he took an axe and tackled the remainder of the logs left in the woodpile. He cut them into stove fitting lengths, cleaved them and stored them away in a nearby shed. My grandfather, watching him from the kitchen window noticed that he worked furiously, but he also noticed one peculiar trait that George Castle had. Every so often he would drop his axe, reach his right hand into his pants pocket and seemingly draw something forth. My grandfather could not see anything in his hand, but apparently George thought that he held something, for a look of sheer horror would cross his face as he gazed at the object invisible to grandfather. Then he would pick up his axe and resume working.

Later, George Castle went into the woods with the other men of the settlement and cut down a winter's supply of firewood. When the first snowfall came and a good slide path was created, George would take my grandfather's ox and slide, haul out the wood and stock it in the pile. The old, familiar, outport woodpile. At that time, not too far from the settlement there were fairly large stands of timber. They have long since been wiped out by over cutting and forest fires.

Castle's companions in the woods and on the trail also noticed that as he cut wood or walked along by the side of the slide, he would put his hand in his pocket, appear to take something out, gaze at it for a few seconds, then go through the motion of throwing it away. None of them ever questioned him about this strange action, they simply reasoned that it was a habit he'd acquired.

George kept working hard all winter hauling out the wood, chopping it, cleaving it and storing it away. He peeled the bark from the sticks saved for fence repairs, attended to the ox, shovelled snow and hauled water. In fact, he never seemed to stop working only to eat and sleep.

In the spring of that year, my grandfather was a very sick man. His arm had shrunk to about half its normal size. I suppose the average doctor today would tell him that he had bone cancer, or some such disease. He would get up each morning, walk the floor back and forth, then sink into his chair in the chimney corner from sheer exhaustion. He grew weaker each day, but very often it took an awful lot of punishment to kill those hardy fishermen. Then near the end of April, after George Castle had finished his day's work, he came into the kitchen and sat down near my grandfather.

"Skipper," said the Englishman, "I'll be leaving you tomorrow. I have finally decided to make my way back to my old home in England. Over the past few years I have managed to put enough money by to pay for the passage."

My grandfather replied, "Well, George, I will be sure enough sorry to lose you. You have been a real good man around here. But George, there is something I always intended asking you about, but I thought that it was none of my business. However, now that you are leaving I'm going to ask you anyway. That habit you have of stopping work every now and then, putting your hand in your pocket, apparently pulling something out, looking at it and then throwing it away."

"Well Skipper, I have a confession to make and you are the first person I ever told this to since that horrible night when this happened forty years ago. You see Mr. Pitman, I am a murderer."

The shock created by Castle's statement caused my grandfather to sit bolt upright in his chair. My grandmother and mother were in the kitchen when the man dropped his bombshell. Grandmother was the first to find her voice.

"George," she said, "you don't look or act like a murderer to me."

"Thank you for that kind remark ma'am, but regardless of what your opinion of me may be, I am a murderer just the same. Now if you will have a little patience with me I will tell you the whole story.

"I was born and raised on my father's farm back in England. I was an only child. The farmer living next to us and whose property was adjoining ours had an only child also, a daughter. She was a year younger than me. I guess that I was in love with her from our school days and when we'd reached our late teens, Stella, that was her name, had developed into a very beautiful young lady. She was tall for a girl, she had long, golden curls and wide, blue eyes. When she was nineteen years old and I was twenty, we became engaged. We planned our wedding to take place after the harvest and when the crops we had to sell were disposed of. Our engagement had the effect of making both of our families happy. My father and mother liked Stella immensely and her parents made no secret of the fact that they would be glad indeed to have me for a son-in-law.

"That year the crops grew well in our locality. My father and I hauled several loads of produce to market in a large seaport town some twenty miles from the farm.

"Late in September my father decided that he would need additional supplies to last us throughout the winter. So he said to me, 'If you start out around sundown, drive through the night, you can reach town early, have a meal, buy the supplies and be home by tomorrow night.' He continued, 'Our old horse knows his way home, so you can catch a nap or two in the wagon on the way back.'

"So I had a shave and changed my clothes. I hitched up the horse and set out. As my fiancee's home was out the road from ours, I naturally called on her. I told her where I was going and when I'd be back. After kissing her goodbye I went on my way a happy man. Our wedding would take place in a week from that day.

"When I was about ten miles out it struck me that I had forgotten the wallet my father had left for me on the kitchen shelf. I couldn't buy supplies without the money in that wallet. So turning around the horse, I headed for home. Of course on the return trip I came to my fiancee's farm first, so I decided to visit her and give her what I was sure would be a real pleasant surprise. Instead of driving through the gate and up to the farmhouse, I tied my horse outside, then walked in the road leading to it. I thought that by moving in silently, her surprise would be greater. As it turned out, it was.

"A grove of trees stood on each side of the farmhouse road. I was half along this road when I heard voices and laughter coming from the direction of the trees on my right. I stood stock still and listened. The voices of a man and a woman came to me clearly. I knew those voices, the woman's was that of my fiancee and the man's was that of the son of the farmer whose premises lay just beyond ours. This man was about my own age, a tall, handsome fellow, who'd earned for himself the reputation of being quite a ladies man, but I never even suspected that Stella and he were having an affair.

"I took off my boots and crept softly through the trees towards the couple. You can pretty well imagine my feelings when there in a little grassy glade I came up on them in the act of making love. I became filled with a rage as cold as ice. I knew then what I was going to do. I would kill them both. Backing away slowly, I circled the grove and came across what I knew I would find, for such implements were always in position ready for use; an axe stuck in a chopping block.

"The sky which had been overcast all along had now cleared and the moon was shining brightly. I circled back again and crept through the grove to find the lovers sitting up with their backs toward me. They had their arms about each other and they were talking and laughing gaily. I wanted them to know who killed them, so I shouted out. They turned about and were struck speechless and motionless with surprise. I am going to kill you both, I told them. The man was making an attempt to rise when I brought the pole of the axe down on the top of his skull, crushing it like an eggshell. The girl opened her mouth as if she were attempting to scream but no sound came. I swung the blade of the axe down towards her head, she ducked to one side and the blade instead of splitting her skull, sheared off a piece of flesh from the side of her head. It stuck to the axe blade and a long, golden curl was attached to it. She lay on the ground moaning. I crushed her skull with the pole of the axe.

"Laying the axe down, I dragged both bodies deep into the grove. I went back and picked up the axe, the piece of flesh still stuck to the blade. I did not remove it. I took the murder weapon back to where the bodies were and covered them up with moss and dead branches.

"I knew that I had to get away from there as quickly as possible and was aware of the fact that I would need money, so I drove back to our farm. No lights showed and I knew that my father and mother were asleep as they always retired early. I sneaked into the house, found the wallet where my father had left it and stuffed it into my pocket. I boarded my wagon and left. When I reached the seaport town I stopped near a wharf where a large square-rigged schooner lay.

"I led my horse behind a shed and tied him. Then I walked out to the side of the ship. Four men stood on deck talking. I announced that I would like to talk to the captain. A tall, powerfully built man stepped forward.

"He said, 'I am the captain, what can I do for you?'

"If your ship is bound for the United States or Canada I'd like to take passage with you. I can pay you for it.

" 'As a matter of fact, we're bound for New York City. We'll be leaving in about twenty minutes. We've got a spare cabin so if you can pay for the voyage as you say, you'll be welcome aboard.'

"I was overjoyed for a piece of luck which I actually felt that I didn't deserve. When I stepped on deck I asked the captain if it was an American ship. But he replied that he and the entire crew were Canadians. I paid him the fare he requested from the money in my father's wallet. I was shown to my cabin and a few minutes later we were under weigh.

"There is no need to go into details about my bouts of seasickness and a couple of storms we'd encountered, suffice to say that we arrived safely in New York. I shook hands with the captain and thanked him for the safe passage, then I took my departure. I walked up town and located lodging where I engaged a room.

"The following morning I was lucky again, for I got a job in a clothing factory. I was assigned to sweeping floors and was instructed to take the sweepings to the furnace room and burn them. That afternoon I swept up, went to the furnace room and threw the trash into the furnace. The regular fireman wasn't present, so I sat down on a bench to have a smoke. As I put my hand into my pocket to get my pipe, I felt my fingers come in contact with something strange. I pulled it out and discovered to my horror that I was holding the section of flesh with the long curl attached which I had shaved off my fiancee's head back in England.

"Yanking open the furnace door, I threw the horrible thing into the flames, but I never got rid of it. It has stayed with me wherever I've roamed, on the prairies, in the mines, on Gloucester fishing vessels out on the Georges Banks. Then one night when I was on deck on the Banks, the girl's hair blew across my nose and nearly smothered me.

"After forty years of suffering that kind of hell, I am going home to turn myself over to the police and make a full admission of the terrible crime I committed so long ago. They may hang me even now and I don't really care. I escaped from the law and the hangman up to now, but I've been paying far too high a price just the same, for I never could manage to escape from the damning curl."

When my family awoke the next morning, George Castle was gone. My grandfather passed away a few days later. My grandmother never did learn what finally happened to George Castle.

Haunted Men: Murray McCune

After my grandfather passed away, my grandmother was left with two teenaged daughters and an eight year old son to raise. But she was a strong, resourceful woman. She owned a fairly large house that had three spare bedrooms upstairs and a room downstairs which she turned into a fourth bedroom. With these she earned a living for herself and her family by taking in boarders. She did very well at this occupation as there were always commercial travellers on the move. Then there were the Jewish and Assyrian peddlers who stayed there from time to time, using Grandmother's house as a base camp and travelling to nearby settlements to display their wares. Carrying huge packs on their backs with a large jewellery box hanging down over their chests, some of those men eventually became very successful St. John's businessmen.

In addition, waves of partridge hunters would arrive from the nearby French town of St. Pierre to engage in hunting those tasty little birds, which were extremely plentiful in those days on the barrens near Lamaline. The French hunters would keep coming until the first snowstorm appeared. Grandmother's bedrooms were seldom vacant. Very often those Frenchmen were obliged to sleep three to a bed, but they didn't mind that in the least. Partridges were their main concern and they usually went home with good bags.

One day in October, a knock sounded on the front door and Grandmother, thinking that someone was seeking lodging answered the summons. On opening the door she observed a man standing there, he was of medium height and was stockily built. That he was elderly she could easily tell. He was wearing a beard and mustache that had once been dark but which now was overshot with grey. A stick rested over one of his shoulders, on the overhang of which a fair sized bundle was suspended.

"What can I do for you?" my grandmother asked.

"Well ma'am," he replied, "as I was entering your town I met a man and asked him if he knew of anyone who would put me up for the winter, give me the necessary meals and a place to sleep. In return for such privileges I would perform any type of work as long and as hard as my benefactor needed me to. I do not seek payment for my toil."

Then he told my grandmother that his name was Murray McCune, that he was an Irishman born, that he had left his home in Ireland forty-one years before and had not been back since.

"The man I told you about directed me to you and I would feel more than obliged to you ma'am, if you could manage to put me up."

Grandmother, remembering George Castle's story and the reason he had left home in such a juice of a hurry, replied, "Before I decide to take you on Mr. McCune, I am going to ask you a question whether you like it or not. Why did you leave Ireland in the first place?"

The man answered, "You see ma'am, I got the urge to come across to this side of the Atlantic, hoping that I might better myself. I'm afraid though I wandered around too much. A sort of rolling stone you might say. And sad to relate, I never gathered much moss."

As the man was polite in his speech and appeared to be gentlemanly enough and as Grandmother needed someone to put in firewood enough for the winter ahead and perform other odds and ends that needed tending, she took McCune on. She thought to herself that if he proved to be no good she could always throw him out.

But Murray McCune did not disappoint her. The very next day he proved himself to be just as good a worker as George Castle. Later in the fall, he went into the woods and cut down a full winter's supply of firewood, which he hauled out through the next four months. In April he spent three days digging up Grandmother's vegetable gardens.

On the evening of May first, he came in and told Grandmother that he would be leaving in the morning.

"Your gardens are all ready for planting and I have cut enough new wood to see you through the summer and fall. I want to move on, however, I think I must return to my home in Ireland.

"I have to admit something to you, I feel I owe you that for your kindness in taking me in. I was not exactly honest with you last fall. I was afraid if I told you the truth you would not have taken me in. You see, I was involved in a double murder back home and it is possible that a third person may have died there. I never stayed around long enough to find out about the third one. Some time ago I decided to tell you the truth when it came time for me to leave and here it is.

"I was born and raised on my father's farm in Northern Ireland. I was the eldest of six children. From the time I was ten years old, I had the hankering to go to the United States or Canada and as soon as I was old enough I was determined that I would go. The day following my nineteenth birthday, I informed my parents that I was leaving home the next day. I told them that I would walk to Belfast and endeavour to secure a job as a hand on some ship that may be bound for one of the foreign countries.

"My father put his hands on my shoulders and said that as I was a young man full grown, if I wanted to leave he wouldn't stand in my way. I expected an outburst from my mother, but she said nothing. Pointing out that there were good wages being paid on the other side of the ocean and that

when I got settled I would be able to send money back to help
them out, they seemed to be content with my leaving.

"The following afternoon I bade farewell to my parents
and my younger brothers and sisters. As my mother pressed
my hand she made no sound, but I noticed tears rolling down
her cheeks. She passed me a package of sandwiches and I left.

"I should say here," continued McCune, "that since I was
a little boy, there have been two things which I fear greatly.
One is thunder and lightening storms and the other is dead
people. When I was a tiny lad, one of our neighbours, a man,
died. My mother took me along when she attended the wake.
She lifted me up to view the corpse and I got such a fright that
I screamed and screamed and had to be removed from the
house. I was still young when one day our house was struck by
lightning, which seemed to come out of the clear sky. Nobody
was hurt but it gave me a terrible scare.

"Anyway, at sundown I came to a small brook that ran
underneath the road. It was a pleasant spot so I sat down on
the brook's bank and ate part of my sandwiches. I took a drink
from the stream and then continued on my way. Several
horses and rigs passed me on the road. None offered me a
ride and I didn't request one. About an hour after I left that
brook, darkness descended. Then one of the menaces that I
dreaded put in an appearance.

"Lightning started to flash around me followed by heavy
claps of thunder, while rain came down in torrents. It was bad
enough for me to be seated in a house while such a storm
raged, but to actually be caught out in the open was pure
terror. At that time, I noticed a twinkle of lights gleaming
faintly off to my right. A light meant a dwelling, very probably
a farmhouse. I would ask the people living there to give me
shelter. I could stay in their barn or other outbuilding until
the storm passed. The thought struck me that perhaps these
people knew my parents which could be of help to me.

"I continued along the road at a trot for a few more yards,

when the lightening revealed to me a rather narrow side road leading off the main road. I then realized that in order to reach the light I would have to walk down the road, which I did. I finally came to a large, white farmhouse where the light was showing through one of its windows on my right hand side. Going up to the front door, I knocked. I received no answer; thinking the occupants might be somewhere at the back of the house, I rapped a little louder, there was still no answer. As the electrical storm was still raging and I needed shelter I gave several hard knocks. The force of the blows caused the door to fly open.

"The open door presented to my view a large room which I judged to be the parlour and right in front of me was my second cause for terror, a coffin rested on two chairs and in that coffin lay the body of a man. The light from a bracket lamp showed his emaciated features quite plainly. I remained rooted to the spot with fear clutching my heart. As it seemed preferable to face the raging storm outside rather than a dead man, I was trying to gather enough strength in my shaky legs to back away when the corpse sat bolt upright.

"If I'd been scared of the dead man, I cannot describe my feelings of horror when he suddenly came erect. My body felt as if it were encased in ice; I was numb. Then the corpse spoke.

" 'Have no fear of me boy,' it said, 'for I'm not really dead.' Reaching down by his side he brought up a revolver. Pointing it at me he ordered, 'Come in and close that door.' Which I did.

" 'Now,' he said, 'I've got a story to tell you and then I will need your help to finish a plan which I have in mind. I'm certainly happy that you happened along. We don't have much time, for as soon as that storm lets up they'll be back.'

"At that time he did not explain who *they* were. Climbing out of the coffin he sat on a chair and motioned for me to sit also.

"He said, 'I'll begin by telling you that my name is Samuel O'Dell, that I am fifty-seven years old and my wife is twenty. So you see I am older than she is by thirty-seven years. She is my second wife. When my first wife became ill I hired this girl to do the cooking and cleaning and to attend on my wife who was bedridden. She's the eldest of a large family who live about three miles from here. She was eighteen when she came here and was happy to do it. Her family being poor, Mary Ann was glad I offered her a job because for the first time in her life she would be well fed and have a bed all to herself to sleep in. Besides, I paid her fairly good wages. Nearly two years after she arrived, my wife died and a month later I proposed to Mary Ann. Oh, she hesitated at first, but when I pointed out that I owned a large, prosperous farm with a fine house and outbuildings and that I would have a will drawn up leaving her everything, she accepted. A week later we were married.

" 'It was about three weeks ago that I discovered she was having an affair with the farmer that owns the property beside mine. He's young and handsome with curly, red hair. His name is Jack Morrissey. Just the type to appeal to Mary Ann. Look at me, I'm short and bald. His parents are dead and he only has an elderly housekeeper around the house, so he has a free hand with his affairs. I did not suspect anything was amiss for a long, long time. Then one day while I was hunting a stray horse I saw my wife come out of a grove of trees between the two properties. I knew then what she was up to, she had been visiting with that handsome farmer.

" 'The next morning I told her I would be working the back section of the farm. Leaving her to do the breakfast dishes I went out, but I did not go very far; instead I hid behind some bushes close to the house. Half an hour later I saw her leave. She made a beeline for the house of the man I suspected of being her lover. Keeping myself hid from view I followed her when she entered the grove of trees. Shortly afterwards Morrissey came. They hugged and kissed and lay down and made love. I boiled over with rage. First I was going to go home and collect my shotgun and put an end to them there and then. But I am the kind of man never to rush into anything too fast. So I backed out of the grove and made my way home. On the way I decided to have a little fun with them before I sent them out of his world.

" 'The following morning when I arose from bed I complained of pains in my stomach. Mary Ann could not quite hide the look of delight in her eyes, she did not suggest I see a doctor. For the next two weeks I willed myself to eat just enough to keep, myself alive; meanwhile, I practised holding my breath and letting the air in and out slowly so it would take a keen eye to notice the rise and fall of my chest.

" 'Early this morning I called my wife to my bedside and told her that I was going, then I gave a groan and became silent, so as far as she could tell I had passed away. She was a very happy widow. The moment I died she ran to her lover's house and they both came back here. I could hear them laughing and talking in the kitchen. They came into my room and he picked me up and carried me into the parlour and dumped me on the floor. Neither of them had the sense to check my pulse or heart beat. He went out to the woodshed and hammered together the rude coffin you found me in. After he had laid me out, they went into the kitchen and cooked a meal. As they ate they made their plans. First they thought to bury me under the manure pile and put it around that I had disappeared, but on second thoughts they decided the neighbours would become suspicious and call in the authorities. It was then Morrissey came up with this idea of throwing my body into a pond by the side of the road tonight and Mary Ann would go to the Magistrate and say I had been missing for three or four days and ask for a search of the area. Of course, I would be found in time floating on the pond. As there would be no signs of violence on my body, they would not be accused of killing me. Both of them left late this afternoon and went to his place, I suppose to indulge in another session of love making.

" 'They were going to return after dark to take me to the pond, but I guess the thunder and lightning storm held them up. Boy', he said, 'I'll need your help after I kill them, but I'll go into that later.' Then he held up his hand.

" 'Listen,' he said, 'the storm is over so they will be back here soon. You go and get in the wardrobe over there by the fireplace. There's a crack across the top part of the panel so you will be able to see what happens.' He grinned maniacally. 'You will have a ring side seat you might say.' He pointed the revolver at me, 'Get into the cupboard right now,' he yelled.

"I did as he directed, entered the cupboard and closed the door; with that gun on me I didn't have a choice. Through the crack in the panel I saw him climb back into the coffin with his revolver and settle down. About fifteen minutes later the front door opened and a tall, handsome man and a pretty woman entered the parlour. They walked over to the coffin and gazed on the supposedly dead man.

" 'Well Samuel, me lad,' said the man, 'me and your charmin' wife have decided to send you on a voyage, good for the health you know.'

" 'Yes,' chimed in the wife, 'it's lovely on the water this time o' year.'

"As she finished speaking, O'Dell propped up like a jack-in-the-box. 'You are both dead,' he croaked and he shot the man between the eyes. The fellow fell backwards out of my line of vision. Mrs. O'Dell raised both hands over her head and started to scream. O'Dell silenced her when he sent a bullet into her throat. She fell and I could hear her choking on her own blood. But she soon became silent.

"O'Dell came out of the coffin and yelled at me to leave the wardrobe. Keeping his gun trained on me he ordered me to drag the bodies to the manure pile.

" 'I am going to bury them in the same place they wanted to put me. Don't you try anything funny either. This gun is an American six shooter a friend sent me from the United States and it still has four bullets in it.'

"I dragged the man's body down first and then the woman's with O'Dell following me along back and forth covering me with the gun. He pointed to a shovel leaning on the wall of the barn and directed me to dig a grave large enough to hold them both. So I dug and when I reached about four feet deep he stopped me.

" 'O'Dell, you have forced me to become an accessory to a double murder.'

" 'Yeah, I know,' he replied, 'but you are a strong, young man and it was easier for you to dig that grave than me in my weakened condition.' Then his gaunt face cracked from ear to ear in a hideous grin. A death's head if ever there was one.

"I realized then that he did not intend for me to leave that place alive, for I was the only witness to his crime. And I guessed that he could not afford to let me go and report the double murder to the police. He ordered me to dump the bodies in the grave, that horrible grin still on his face as if he were enjoying some private joke. I now had a good idea what was causing his amusement. I was sure that the moment I'd placed the murdered pair in that hole, he intended to shoot me and pile me down on top of them. Then I got O'Dell to fall for one of the oldest ruses known to man.

"I shouted, 'O'Dell, look out behind you!'

"He wheeled about, surprisingly fast for a man who was supposed to be weakened from self starvation. As he swung about, his revolver swung with him and I walloped him across the back of the head with the flat of the shovel blade. He fell forwards and landed on his face on top of the pile of earth I had dug, his gun flew out of his hand and landed at my feet. The loose earth on which he fell slid back into the grave and O'Dell went down with it and disappeared. I only paused long enough to pick up the revolver and throw it as far away as I could. I didn't know if O'Dell was simply injured or dead and I never remained there long enough to find out. I ran out of the farmyard and down his private road onto the main highway. I slowed then to a walk, confident that even if the farmer was alive he would be in no condition to pursue me.

"I knew that it was essential for me to get away from Ireland as I did not want to be caught and charged with a double or possibly a triple murder or of being an accessory either. I reached Belfast without further incident and I was lucky enough to find a job on a square-rigger as a cook's helper. I signed on and the next day we were outward bound for Montreal.

"When we reached that Canadian port I left ship and have been wandering all over North America ever since. Now I'm tired of drifting and I am going home and tell my story to the authorities. After that I guess it will up to them."

McCune thanked my grandmother for taking him in. The next morning he left for good.

Haunted Men: Jonathan Lovell

At the end of the following year, bless me if another drifter didn't run up and apply to my grandmother for a winter's lodging. He gave his name as Jonathan Lovell. He was an Englishman who had left his home in England thirty years earlier and had never returned. He gave his age as fifty-one and stated that he had been wandering from place to place all over the United States and Canada.

"Could never seem to settle down, ma'am."

He had arrived in Newfoundland in March, he told Grandmother and had signed on a Banks fishing schooner sailing out of Burin. When the voyage had ended at the end of October, he had collected his wages and made his way to Grand Bank. After spending his money and whiling away his time in Grand Bank he had decided to move on so he had walked to Lamaline.

Lovell was a little man, five feet, five inches tall and slightly built. He was polite and mannerly and his face carried a cheerful grin. Unlike his predecessors he requested a small wage and room and board for any work he performed. He said that he was quite willing to do any task he was able. Then Grandmother shot this double question at him.

"Mr. Lovell, why did you leave home in the first place and why have you not since returned?"

"Well, ma'am," replied the cheerful Jonathan, "after I grew up I thought to myself that I should like to see other parts of the world. I never went back home because I never really felt an urge to."

Grandmother, of course, in the light of what she learned

from Castle and McCune did not believe him. However, she told Lovell, "I've decided to take you on, but remember this, if you do not measure up, out you go."

She then instructed my young uncle Bob to show Jonathan to his room in the attic. The same room that had been occupied by the other Englishman and the Irishman.

The following day, Jonathan Lovell, despite his small size and light weight, proved himself to be just as able a worker as Castle and McCune. So the winter passed with this man performing all chores nobly and well.

To go back to the second day after the new man had arrived. During the midday meal, he performed an act which although it didn't upset my grandmother in the least, greatly disturbed my mother and her younger sister, Aunt Emily. Jonathan Lovell, like the two men before him, was allowed to take his dinner with the family in the large kitchen. They were seated around the table enjoying their meal, when suddenly Lovell dropped his knife and fork with a clatter and batted at his shoulders with both hands, shouting, "Get away from there, get away from there."

After a while, he picked up his knife and fork and resumed eating. As no member of the family could see anything on the man's shoulders which would cause his violent actions and shouting, Grandmother asked him what he was slapping and yelling about.

"It's little devils ma'am, is what I was driving away. You see ma'am, they always perch on my shoulders when I'm taking my meals and tickle my ears. Most annoying they are. Could you folks see them?" enquired Mr. Lovell.

"No," replied Grandmother testily. "We couldn't see them because they weren't there. I think they are just a product of your imagination."

"Oh they perch there alright," said Jonathan, "I see them plain enough even if you can't."

And that was the only thing that appeared to be abnormal

about Jonathan Lovell, and that was plenty as far as my mother and aunt were concerned. After the man had returned to work the two daughters went to their mother.

"Mom, you have to get rid of that man."

"Why?" asked Grandmother.

"Well, you saw what he did at the table," said Mother.

"Yes," chimed in Aunt Emily, "he also insisted that he could actually see those devils, the man is insane."

"No, I will not get rid of him, we need him too badly to do the work that needs to be done on the premises during the winter. Personally, I think Jonathan was just having a bit of fun for himself, putting on that devil batting act to scare you young people."

As the winter wore on, Lovell would put on his devil driving away show two or three days a week, usually at midday or at supper time. One day his shouting and batting became exceptionally violent. After he had gone outside my mother and aunt descended on Grandmother like a northeast gale.

"Lovell has got to go," insisted my mother. "When those devils overcome him, he's totally insane. Do you want us all to be murdered in our beds?"

"No, of course not," replied Grandmother. "But you must remember that Jonathan Lovell has never laid a hand on or attempted in any way to harm any member of this family. That little act he puts on at mealtimes, well, it had done us no hurt; let him have his fun, I say."

Uncle Bob sided with his mother, he didn't want Jonathan to leave either, for the little man was always carving out things from blocks of wood for him to play with, like boats, spin tops and so on. My mother and aunt knew it was useless to argue the point any further with Grandmother. They did, however, take the precaution of barricading their bedroom door every night.

Around the middle of April the family arose one morning to find that Lovell had disappeared. He left no word as to where he was heading. If the little man had had a gruesome story to tell connected to his former life, as Grandmother always suspected, he never told it.

One might ask why it was that drifters seeking lodging for the winter always turned up at my grandmother's door. Why did those individuals select this residence above all others? Well, I think that can be explained by the fact that my grandmother was born and raised in Grand Bank and at that time she had several brothers and sisters as well as many relatives and friends living there. So the wanderers, who in all three cases, had arrived at Grand Bank first, and enquired around about the possibility of securing a berth for the winter, more than likely asked it of a relative or friend of grandmother's. They, being fully aware of the family's needs, would naturally direct aid to them. Thus it was that the drifters found accommodation with my grandmother.

My Slippery Stick

The night was clear with heavy frost,
As I trudged along the road,
And the way was all with ice embossed,
So my walk got kind of slowed.
When near the brook I sought about
To see if I could find
Some sort of staff to help me out,
To keep my legs untwined.

Then very soon I found a stick,
That appeared to me quite good,
I was sure that it would do the trick
For it seemed of stoutish wood.
So with its aid I reached my home
And threw it behind the stove,
As sleep was clouding up my dome
I off to bed did rove.

When I was waked by piercing screams,
The sun was soaring high,
To learn what had disturbed my dreams
I down the stairs did fly.
My wife was standing on a chair,
Her face with terror shot.
While her mother pranced like a circus mare,
On the stove which glowed red hot.

They both were pointing at the floor,
Uttering language strange to me,
I downward glanced and by the door
All plain for me to see,
Was my trusty staff of yesternight,
Now came my turn to squeal,
For wriggling there in sheer delight
Was my stick: A thawed out eel!

The Ghost of Little Lawn

Do I believe in ghosts? Well I didn't, not for a long, long time. Then in the month of January 1935, an incident occurred, a personal experience which caused my ideas of being a non-believer in ghostly visitations to undergo a complete state of revision. Over the years prior to the date mentioned above, I had heard several people relate how when walking along lonely roads late at night they encountered ghosts and in every case the story tellers hadn't been ashamed to admit that as soon as they'd eyed the visitors from another world, they promptly departed the scene with all the speed they could command. On hearing those yarns I took note of the fact that the experiences had occurred after darkness had descended. Why, I would argue, if there are ghosts how is it they never put in a scattered appearance during daylight?

In 1935, I was a member of the Newfoundland Constabulary; Newfoundland was under Commission of Government. The Department of Public Health and Welfare was administered by Sir John Puddister, one of the Newfoundland Commissioners. It seemed that Sir John had been receiving unfavourable reports concerning the methods by which some of the outport relieving officers were handling matters. In some cases these officials were issuing relief to people not in need while other people who were actually hungry failed to get the necessary aid. Sir John decided that there was only one way to prove or disprove those reports and that was to appoint several members of the Newfoundland Constabulary as relief inspectors and have them check on each and every family who was then on the dole and on any others who may be applying for it.

Accordingly, with the cooperation of the Commissioner for Justice and the Chief of Police, fifteen members of the force, including myself, were ordered to report to Sir John Puddister at a certain hour on a specific day. P.J. O'Neill, the Police Chief, when giving us that order, informed us that until we received instructions to the contrary we would be under the control of the Commissioner for Public Health and Welfare.

When we reported in to the Commissioner he lectured us for upwards of an hour, his main theme being the sins of commission and omission that were reportedly committed by certain relieving officers.

"I am depending on you men," boomed Sir John, "to send in or bring me in true and detailed accounts on conditions in the areas you visit."

My first assignment was to cover a number of settlements situated at the bottom of two bays; namely, Trinity and Placentia. First I was instructed to handle the Trinity Bay section, then cross the three mile neck of land which separated that bay from Placentia Bay and go on from there. After I'd gone over each section thoroughly, I returned to St. John's and handed in my report to Dr. H.M. Mosdell who was the Assistant Commissioner for Public Health and Welfare. The doctor informed me that he would study it, then pass it on to Sir John Puddister for his perusal and comments.

"By the way," said Dr. Mosdell, "I want you to come in at 2:00 p.m. tomorrow, as I have a special assignment for you that will take you somewhat west of your present territory. I will give you all the details when you report in tomorrow."

When I arrived at Dr. Mosdell's office the following afternoon, he told me, "I've received a letter from Lawn. I don't have much respect for the letter or its writer, for the reason that he or she did not sign a name to it. As a rule," he said, "I throw such anonymous missives into the waste basket, but on reading the letter over a second time I've decided to act on it. This letter," he went on, "tells of a number of residents of Lawn who have been receiving able bodied relief since last fall when they actually don't need it. Furthermore, the letter states that these characters have a large supply of different types of food stuffs hidden underneath the hay in their barns and some of them have sacks of flour and other items hidden underneath their codtraps and other type nets in their waterfront storage places.

"About two years ago," continued the doctor, "we appointed Verneau Turpin of St. Lawrence as relieving officer for that section. He struck me as a very sturdy, intelligent and reliable individual. Lawn, of course, is one of the places where Mr. Turpin dispenses able bodied relief. He does not go up there to issue the dole notes, the people needing assistance come down to St. Lawrence to collect them. Verneau Turpin," continued Dr. Mosdell, "was born and raised in that area and he knows every person applying for relief personally. Consequently, I find it hard to believe that a group of men could possibly keep on fooling him for so long a time. However," said the doctor, "I want you to go up there and check it out." He passed me over the letter, "Take that along," he said. "Let Turpin read it, he may possibly recognize the writing."

I arrived at St. Lawrence via the coastal steamer *Argyle* on the forenoon of January 4, 1935. Constable Victor Mullett of the Constabulary stationed at St. Lawrence was on the wharf when the steamer docked. He accompanied me to the boarding house, after which I visited and interviewed the relieving officer. Verneau Turpin was a man in his mid thirties, he was around six feet in height and was powerfully built. I passed him over the anonymous letter; he read it and studied it for a while, then he went to a filing cabinet and brought forth all the applications of every person who had applied for able

bodied relief. We both examined those applications thor-
oughly comparing the writing on them with the writing in the
letter and although we weren't handwriting experts, it was
very obvious that the letter writer had never made out an
application for relief. Of course, it was possible that he or she
might have been on relief and could have gotten a friend or
a relative who was not on the rolls to write it. Mr. Turpin and
I decided that we would pay a visit to Lawn the following
morning. The relieving officer told me that he would borrow
his father's pony and slide for us to make the trip. We also
agreed to leave fairly early, so at seven o'clock the next
morning, Turpin called for me at my boarding house and we
set out.

About an inch of snow had fallen during the night. There
was a very light breeze blowing from the northwest and it was
freezing hard. The fresh snowfall made a good slide path,
and although that sturdy, little black pony was no race horse,
he took us along at a steady trot so we made the ten miles to
Lawn in very good time.

We immediately interviewed the heads of the five families
mentioned in the letter and advised them of its contents.
Fortunately, Verneau knew where they all lived so we didn't
lose any time in locating them. I told them point blank that
the facts contained in the letter damned them as persons
receiving the dole under false pretences. They replied that if
they weren't in need they would not have applied for relief in
the first place. Of course, one would hardly expect them to
admit to the charges. I informed them that it would be
necessary for Mr. Turpin and myself to make a thorough
search of the premises in order to clear their names or
otherwise. They instantly agreed to us making a search, in
fact they seemed to welcome such a move.

A minute search through all the premises uncovered no
hidden catches of food, which convinced the relieving officer
and myself that the letter writer was either an evil trouble-

maker or that it was a person who bore some grudge against all five families. The searches had taken considerable time, so by the time we had lunch it was 2:30 p.m. before we left Lawn for the return trip.

The slide on which we were riding was the typical outport wood slide which was used by the senior Turpin for getting out fence material and firewood. Verneau had had the foresight to nail a two by seven plank between the front and back cross beams. We straddled this plank and sat on it with our feet resting on the runners on either side.

As Verneau was driving he was seated up front with me close behind him. The wind was still very light, but it was pretty frosty because Turpin had the tips of both forefingers frozen through his gloves while he was handling the reins. We took the steep hill leading out of the town and finally were on the downgrade heading towards Little Lawn. I don't know what the present situation is at Little Lawn (1986) but at the time of our experience this harbour was totally uninhabited. According to the law at that time you were supposed to drive on the left hand side of the road. But Verneau Turpin for some reason known only to himself drove all the way down that long grade on the right had side.

I did not call his attention to this breach because there was no traffic on the road but ourselves. Our pony was jogging along at a slow trot. We reached a section where a line of young trees were growing all along and tight to the roadside. They ranged in height,from approximately six to eight feet. Sometime earlier somebody had cut a couple of slide loads of those young trees possibly for fencing material, as they were a good size for pickets. This left a vacancy in the tree line, forming a small clearing. I recall that Turpin and I were talking about that vile person; the anonymous letter writer. Turpin was saying how shocking it was for someone to want to injure his neighbours in that way and I was agreeing with him.

We were now opposite the clearing and all conversation instantly ceased for a man was standing right in the centre of it. He stood bolt upright with his hands by his sides like a soldier at attention. He was wearing a dark suit, but no overcoat. His hands were ungloved, but neither Turpin nor I could recall later if he was wearing a hat.

The jogging pony soon took us out of sight of him, our view being blocked by the trees on the outer edge of the clearing, but we both turned to each other and yelled simultaneously, "Did you see that man?!" We both agreed that we had. Indeed it would have been difficult for us not to have seen him as the snowfall of the previous night had covered the ground and every branch of every tree with a dazzling mantle. So the man in the dark suit stood out starkly visible against that background.

I, thinking that the man had stepped off the road to get out of the way of our pony, looked back and told Verneau to stop.

"Why?"

"Because," I said, "that man has not stepped back onto the road yet, which means he probably needs our assistance."

Again I yelled at Verneau to stop which he did. I told him I had to go back and find out what was wrong with the man.

Verneau said, "I wouldn't if I was you and besides I think you would be wasting your time."

"Mr. Turpin," I replied, "here you are, you the relieving officer and me a police officer and we don't return to see if that man needs assistance. If he is found dead there this evening or tomorrow morning, I for one would never forgive myself."

Now it was three o'clock in the afternoon, broad daylight, with the sun occasionally peeping through the clouds. The thought of a ghost never entered my mind. For like I said before, all the ghosts I'd heard people tell about were seen at night and were dressed in robes of spotless white. But our man in his dark suit appeared very unghostlike. So with that beautiful daylight and with a husky man for company, I did not entertain one solitary vestige of fear for anything supernatural.

I got off the slide and told Verneau, "I'm going back there and if I should need your help, I'll call out."

"Please yourself about going back," growled the relieving officer. "But as for me, I'm staying right here."

So back I went and when I reached the clearing there was no man standing there. Then I got the surprise and shock of my life and little slivers of ice that weren't exactly caused by the bitter cold raced up and down my spine. I guess I imagined it, but the fur cap seemed to be lifting off the top of my head. For there were no footprints in the snow where the man had been standing and no footprint trail led in or out of the clearing. Considerably deflated and somewhat stunned, I returned to where I had left the relieving officer. When I drew near, he called, "You didn't find him, did you?"

"No," I replied, "there are no footprints in the snow either."

Turpin said, "I tried to talk you out of going back there for the reason that if you'd seen that man face to face, the sight of him might have turned your blood."

"Verneau," I asked him, "do you know something about that place that I don't?"

"Yes, there are a number of people who claim that they've seen a ghost at that particular spot and there is a story connected with it. As far as I am concerned, I've travelled over this road dozens of times but have never seen anything worse than myself, until today that is."

"Well," I said to Verneau as we jogged homeward, "if there is a story how about letting me hear it."

"No," he replied, "I won't. Kelland, you are a contrary, stubborn man and if I did tell you the story, you probably wouldn't believe me anyway. But," continued Mr. Turpin, "I will make a suggestion to you. The man you are boarding with, Uncle Charlie Beck, was around when a certain happening occurred. He knows the story and I'm sure he will tell it to you if you ask him."

We arrived back in St. Lawrence without further incident. After supper when Uncle Charlie and I were seated in his living room, I asked him if he had ever heard of any person seeing anything unusual on the road that passes Little Lawn.

"If you mean a ghost," he said "I've heard a number of people who claim to have seen one there."

I then told him what I had found or rather what I didn't find after I went back to the clearing. I looked at Mr. Beck expecting him to burst out laughing, but his face remained sober. Getting up he walked over to the calendar hanging on the wall and studied it for a while.

"January the fifth," he said more to himself than to me. "That could be it."

He came back and sat down. Then he said, "I was about fifteen years old when it happened. One day a middle aged man, named Bobby Walsh, who was the maintenance man and caretaker for the R.C. priest, Reverend Father Whelan, was walking from St. Lawrence to Lawn when he was overtaken by a severe blizzard. He smothered and froze to death. There were several bad snowstorms after that and drifts were piled high everywhere. Although search parties went out every day that weather permitted, Mr. Walsh's body was not located until after the snow had melted in the spring. I recall well enough," continued Mr. Beck, "that the tragedy occurred just after New Year's Day. It could have been on this date, January fifth. So its possible that you and Verneau Turpin arrived at the spot where he died on the anniversary and hour of his passing."

The Strange Case of Captain Strickland

Captain Jack Strickland was the owner and skipper of a trim, forty ton schooner. He was a sturdily built man in his mid forties, a resident of the north side of Lamaline situated on the Burin Peninsula. He was married, but had no children. He used his vessel a few times to engage in dory handlining on the Banks. But mainly he followed the coasting trade. Very often he would visit settlements along the coast and pick up a load of dried codfish from small storekeepers which had been taken in trade from shore fishermen in their area. This fish he would convey to St. John's and return with a load of goods for the little merchant. Occasionally he would voyage to North Sydney and pick up a load of coal for some businessman. Then again he would visit Prince Edward Island and return with a load of produce.

One evening in the early fall of 1875, Captain Strickland returned from P.E.I. with the usual load of vegetables. It was nearing sundown when his schooner entered the home harbour and dropped anchor just offshore from the captain's residence.

Jack Strickland was the type of man who was liked by everyone, but he had three special friends who grew up with him. Whenever those men observed Jack's schooner entering the harbour they would gather at his residence to await his arrival. The three men were seated around the kitchen table and Mrs. Strickland was busily preparing a meal for her husband.

When Captain Strickland entered, he stood just inside

the door and greeted his wife and friends. One of the men, Robert Pitman, yelled, "Gracious, what did you do Jack, fall overboard?"

"No," replied Strickland. "Why?"

"Dammit man, you must have," said Pitman. "Your clothes are soaking wet and the water is falling off them and forming pools at your feet."

Captain Jack, Mrs. Strickland and the other two men laughed at this announcement.

"Bob," said one of the men, "you ought to see a doctor, for you're beginnin' to see things that none of us can see."

Bob Pitman walked over and felt Strickland's clothes. "Here is a peculiar thing," he said. "I could see Jack's clothes just as plain as I can see every person and object in this room; now his clothes are dry and the water has disappeared. It certainly is a puzzler."

At this Captain Strickland reached into his mackinaw pocket and drew forth a bottle of Frecker's best rum, for he had touched into St. Pierre on his way home.

"Here Bob," he said, "have a snort of this, it should be good for what's wrong with your eyes."

All the men had a round of drinks and soon after the wet clothes and the forming pools of water that Robert Pitman said he had seen were forgotten. When he had arrived home Captain Strickland was wearing a pair of heavy knee length lace up boots; after he'd had his drink he unlaced his boots and kicked them off, then sat down and had his supper. After Mrs. Strickland had cleared the table, the four men sat around it to play a game of forty-fives. Auction forty-fives or one hundred and twenties had not been invented up to that time.

As one of the men was dealing the cards for the first game, Captain Strickland sprang to his feet.

"Good heavens," he exclaimed. "I forgot to bring Aunt Mary's medicine ashore."

Aunt Mary was a little old lady who lived on the north side, not too far from Captain Strickland. It appears that Aunt Mary had been ailing for several years, complaining of pains here and there, unable to get a good night's sleep and so on. The local doctor had prescribed for her many times, but his medicines had done her very little good, she reported. Then one of her relatives, while on a trip to St. Pierre, visited the French doctor there and described her symptoms to him, with the result that he sent her down a bottle of medicine which he'd made up himself. After taking a few slurps of the Frenchman's medicine Aunt Mary declared it was doing her a world of good. She had hardly any pain now and she was sleeping much better. Aunt Mary had heard that Captain Strickland was going to Prince Edward Island and figuring that he would visit St. Pierre either on the way up or on the return voyage, she sent her grandson with a note to the captain requesting that when he touched in at St. Pierre would he visit the French doctor and get her medicine refilled.

"Jack," she further requested, "promise me that you will deliver that medicine or have it sent to me as soon as you get home."

Captain Jack said to the boy, "Son, tell your grandmother that she's got my word, I'll get the medicine to her as soon as I reach port."

"Boys," Strickland told his friends, "I've got to go back aboard the schooner and get that medicine."

Mrs. Strickland and his three friends pleaded with him to let it wait until morning. "Yes Jack," said his wife, "I'm sure that Aunt Mary will survive the night without the medicine."

"You know," replied the captain, "I never broke my word to anyone yet and I'm certainly not going to begin with Aunt Mary. I gave my word that I would see that she got her medicine as soon as I'd arrived home and I mean to stick to it. Anyway," he continued, "it will only take fifteen or twenty minutes to go back to the vessel and return here. And Hannah, you can take the medicine down to Aunt Mary. Our card game can wait that long and I'll feel a lot happier when I've completed this little job."

So despite further protests from his wife, Jack pulled on his heavy boots, but did not take the time to relace them, grabbed his hat and mackinaw and went out the door. When an hour had passed away and Jack had not returned, Mrs. Strickland and his friends became worried. One of the men surmised that Jack had taken the medicine down to Aunt Mary himself and that was what was delaying him. Robert Pitman said nothing but his mind went back to the vision he'd had of the wet clothes and the pools of water.

After a few more minutes all three men decided to go down to the beach to see if the captain's dory had returned. She had returned alright, as they soon learned when they reached the landwash. She was empty and there was no sign of Captain Strickland. That in itself wouldn't have been too alarming but for one thing which all three noticed, the dory's painter was coiled and resting inboard. They knew that no schoonerman or doryman would land and leave his dory unsecured. If Captain Strickland had landed in that dory, her painter would have been brought ashore and tied securely to one of the posts on the bank. There was a light breeze blowing towards the land. The men were confident that the dory had drifted ashore on her own.

It was a nice night, there was no moon, but the weather was clear. The three men boarded the dory, shoved off and rowed out to the schooner, no words were spoken. On reaching the vessel they clambered aboard; walking along the rail they instantly discovered an object hanging outboard from a belaying pin set in the main rail. When they saw this object it mutely informed them that never again would they play a game of forty-fives with their friend Jack Strickland.

The object was one of the captain's boots and it became very clear to the men what had occurred.

Captain Strickland on boarding his schooner had gone to the cabin, collected Aunt Mary's medicine and returned on deck. He had untied his dory, coiled her painter and threw it aboard. Then as he was springing into the smaller boat, the loose laces of one of his boots slipped down over the belaying pin, holding up one of his feet. The result being that the skipper plunged head first into the water, then when his foot slipped out of the boot on the rail, he went under completely. One of his friends suggested that when he went down first, his head had probably come into violent contact with the dory's hardwood gunnel which had rendered him unconscious and that he'd drowned before he came to. The men knowing there was nothing they could do to attempt to recover the body before daylight, rowed ashore and broke the sad news to Mrs. Strickland.

My mother told me that she was ten years old at the time of the tragedy and that she was asleep in her bedroom in her parents home not too far away from the Strickland property. She was awakened by a woman's violent, agonized screams. The following morning she learned that Captain Strickland had been drowned and that it was his wife who had been screaming after she had been informed of her husband's fate.

Captain Strickland's body was recovered early next morning. There was a large bruise on his forehead which proved that his friend had been right when he thought that the captain's head had struck the dory's gunnel on the way down.

Robert Pitman was a man who enjoyed the respect of his friends and neighbours, he was not given to uttering false-hoods they asserted. So when Pitman repeated several times that he had very clearly seen Captain Strickland's clothes streaming water which formed into pools at his feet, everyone believed him. Many people claimed he had been granted a vision which enabled him to see what was not visible to the other four occupants of the room. A warning to Captain Strickland, as it were, not to venture out on the water again that night.

Incidentally, Robert Pitman was the father of Richard Pitman, the young man who was successful in capturing the Ball Ghost.

Mighty Samson

Policeman Samson changed his duds
To try and find out who
Had stolen Mr. Whelan's spuds
Way back in twenty-two.
He'd found a suspect right away
But did not search his place
For well he knew it does not pay
To suffer loss of face.

Supposing that he'd found spuds there?
In numbers large or small
The man who'd lost them could not swear
He'd owned those spuds at all.
For tubers are so much akin
In peel and eye and look
I think they're mine, would be too thin
For any judge's book.

But Samson persevered and sought
For days without relief
To come up with some better thoughts
To aid him nab the thief.
Then like a star shell in the sky
A bright idea came
Though slim the chance, 'twas worth a try
And Samson was quite game.

The hour was late, the night was dark
With very heavy rain
When Samson hurried to embark
This product of his brain.
He up to Whelan's cellar went
And stayed three hours or more
An infant dawn was seeking vent
When he came out of the door.

That day he spread the word around
He was going up the shore
To do some work in Random Sound
And that he'd come back no more.
But to Whelan he confided that
He was going to a shack
That was owned by Mr. Harvey Pratt
Just five miles down the track.

"Now if your spuds are robbed tonight
And I'm pretty sure they'll be
Perhaps our thief will get a fright —
But get the news to me."
Samson was right, the spuds were robbed
And he was notified
So up to the suspect's house he lobbed
Exactly at noontide.

Still hoping things would work out right
And counting on his hunch
His eyes beheld a welcome sight
The board was set for lunch.
Potatoes dry were steaming there
With cabbage, duff and beef
And beaming angelic air
Sat the man he thought a thief.

The suspect and his charming wife
Both showed a sickly grin
As the constable picked up a knife
And promptly started in.
To cut each homely spud in two
With haste he plied the blade
Then to the couple roared, "Here, you!
Is one mistake you've made.

"Two nights ago I did some work
To spoil your thieving game
I walked though mud and rain and murk
But it paid off just the same
For in the centre of each spud
Here lies a Seadog Match
That really make you out a dud
And help me land a catch."

After Samson had related
How he had caught the thief
The farmer, who was elated
Said, "That's most beyond belief.
You sure deserve a lot of praise
But I just thought of something too
You can be thankful all your days
That they wasn't cut up for stew."

Good Heavens You're a Black Man

During the summer of 1880, several stores along the St. John's waterfront had been broken and entered with various types of merchandise being carried off by the thief or thieves. Quite naturally the Water Street merchants were up in arms and complaining bitterly of the inefficiency of the Newfoundland Constabulary, because after several weeks of thievery the Force had not caught up with and jailed the offenders.

It appeared that the break and enter artists operated after midnight. The police on day duty ended their patrol at eleven p.m. but before they retired, they made a check of all the stores and each time found them intact. The night watch coming on duty at eleven p.m. also checked the stores between eleven p.m. and twelve midnight and learned that no breaks had been made. It was obvious therefore, that the thieves conducted their activities between the hours of midnight and six a.m., for it was during duty hours that the night watch on rechecking the stores had discovered the breaks.

At that time in the life of the Constabulary only four men could be spared for night duty and they always patrolled in pairs. Two of these officers were detailed to patrol the western section of town, that is to say from Adelaide Street west. The other two covered the section east of Adelaide Street. Instructions in the police manual directed that policemen were to visit all streets, courts, lanes and alleys connected to their beats during their tour of duty. Therefore, to be fair to those four men it was not only Water Street that they were required to protect, it was, in short, the whole town. The Water Street section of St. John's was at that time illuminated by gas lamps, mere jets that threw a very feeble circle of light around. Consequently, on pitch dark nights unless people were standing directly underneath those lamps, it was almost impossible to discern them. So we've got to admit that the old time cops had a lot of cards stacked against them. The night watch was supervised by an N.C.O., who was supposed to visit his men as often as possible during his shift.

It was ten minutes before eleven o'clock on a Sunday night, near the end of September 1880, that Sergeant James Lacey ordered his men of the night watch to fall in for instructions. In his remarks Lacey made strong references to the considerable number of breaks, enters and thefts that had occurred in recent weeks. So he instructed the men to be especially on alert and to do all in their power to try and locate and arrest the guilty parties. As Sergeant Lacey was about to turn the men out, Head Constable John Sullivan walked into the police station. When Mr. Sullivan entered he told Sergeant Lacey to hold the men awhile as he had something he wished to say to them. The head constable appeared to be somewhat angry, his ire was probably caused by the drubbing he'd taken from the suffering merchants. He ranted and raved for a while concerning all the robberies which had taken place, then he drove home the dagger.

"I believe," he said, "that many of you men are lacking in courage, that you are turning a blind eye when you observe suspicious characters loitering around the street who may have felonious intentions.

"Now," continued Mr. Sullivan, "I am going to demand more action, tonight and for every night hereafter; if you men see any person loitering on the streets particularly after midnight, whether they be male or female, you will place them under arrest and lock them up here. I will attend to such characters in the morning."

With that Sullivan nodded to Lacey, who immediately ordered the four men to go out and take up their duties. The two constables who Sergeant Lacey had selected to patrol the eastern section of town were Albert Kelland, the senior man, a first cousin of my father, and George Nolan, a recruit constable. It was Nolan's first time on night watch.

At 2 a.m. the two policemen were walking west on Water Street. They had passed the foot of McBrides Hill and as they came in sight of the gas light on the corner of Beck's Cove, they observed two men loitering right underneath it. As they neared the loiterers both of them turned their backs to the policemen and started to walk west on Water Street. Kelland called out for them to halt, the men ignored the order and increased their pace. For a second time Kelland shouted to them to halt, but instead of stopping they both broke into a run; the officers gave chase, Kelland remembering Head Sullivan's order to place under arrest all persons found loitering on the streets after midnight.

He said to Nolan, "We've got to catch them!"

As the two suspects reached the foot of Adelaide Street one of them turned up that street, the other one continued to run west on Water Street. Saying that he would follow the one on Adelaide Street, Kelland shouted to Nolan to continue after the one on Water. Kelland's man reached the head of Adelaide Street and turned east onto Duckworth Street. Constable Kelland noticed that his quarry appeared to be slowing considerably, so he put on an extra burst of speed and caught his man where Duckworth Street and Theatre Hill join. Kelland thought he'd gotten a very good grip on the fellow's arm but suddenly the prisoner broke free. But instead of running away he darted one of his hands towards his hip pocket. Thinking that the man intended to use a weapon of some kind, the constable brought his baton down hard on the fellow's elbow which brought a grunt of pain from him. The policeman seized the man's arm again.

He yelled, "Why were you loitering on the street and why

didn't you halt when I ordered you?" The man made no reply.

In a house across the street some person who had been awakened by the commotion lighted a lamp and shone it out of the bedroom window trying to ascertain what all the fuss was about down below. A glimmer from the lamp flashed across the prisoner's face which Kelland observed was coal black.

"Good heavens," the officer exclaimed, "you're a black man!"

At the time there were a number of French and Spanish ships in port and many of the captains of such ships employed black men who usually served in the capacity of cooks. From previous contact with some of them Kelland knew that not many of them could speak or understand a word of English.

"Whether you can understand me or not, you are now under arrest and I am taking you to the police station."

The policeman was in the act of moving his right hand from the man's upper arm down to his wrist in order to get a better grip when the black man gave a violent lurching twist and once more broke free. Instantly he again darted a hand towards his hip pocket. It was then that Albert Kelland decided to take no further chances, whereupon he struck the man a hard blow on the forehead with his heavy hardwood baton and the prisoner dropped without a sound, apparently out cold.

Kelland bent down and felt the fellow's forehead where the baton had connected. His hand came away very wet and sticky, so he knew that the wound was bleeding pretty badly. He took out his handkerchief and bound it around the injured place. Right then the man on the ground moaned and spoke in perfect English, "My God, Kelland, you've killed me."

Kelland recognized that voice all too well, because the

man he'd clubbed so severely was none other than Head
Constable John Sullivan. It seems that after the night watch
had gone out, Sullivan had returned to his house and
changed into civilian clothes. He'd trimmed off his beard,
blackened his face and hands with soot from the kitchen
stove, then went on the prowl. After discovering who he'd laid
low, the policeman was at first horrified, then he became
angry.

"Head Constable, you were undoubtedly sneaking
around in civilian clothes with your face blackened to see how
well we were performing our duty and in the meantime
putting on running away to learn if we had the guts to capture
you. Well sir, I'm afraid now that you have gained all the
knowledge you need in that respect. Sir," continued the
policeman, "why didn't you identify yourself when I caught
you or when I struck your elbow with my baton?"

Sullivan made no reply. At that moment Sergeant Lacey
and Constable Nolan arrived on the scene. Lacey, not being
aware that Sullivan had been rather severely injured was
laughing and seemed to be enjoying himself. Lacey too, was
dressed in civilian clothes and had his face and hands black-
ened. Lacey's merriment caused Albert Kelland to become
more angry, so he turned on his N.C.O.

"Look Sergeant," he shouted, "this is no laughing matter,
for I nearly killed the Head Constable with my baton."

On hearing this Lacey became concerned and in the
darkness did his best to examine the extent of Sullivan's
injury.

"I think, sir," he said to his superior officer, "that we
should take you to a doctor."

"No need of that," Sullivan replied. "Just assist me down
to the police station."

The police station at that time was situated at the back of
the old General Post Office on George Street. The three men
literally carried the Head Constable to the station where

Kelland's blood soaked handkerchief was removed and the wound washed clean. The cut from the baton wallop was about two inches long and fairly deep. Again Sergeant Lacey suggested sending for a doctor as he said in his opinion the cut needed to be stitched. But Sullivan would have none of it.

"Put a bandage on the wound," he instructed. "Then assist me to my house at Fort Townshend."

There was an elderly constable on guard at the police station and before he left, Head Sullivan called all four officers to come to where he was sitting. He told them sternly that under no circumstances was either of them to divulge what had happened.

"This incident," he impressed upon them, "must remain a secret between the five of us."

Then with Constable Kelland holding him up by one arm, Constable Nolan holding him up by the other and with Sergeant Lacey following along behind, they got the injured man home and helped Mrs. Sullivan in putting him to bed. When the three officers were leaving, Sullivan said, "Don't worry about this little cut. It will heal in a while and my wife is good at administering to such injuries."

Now to come back to Sergeant Lacey and Constable Nolan. Lacey, of course, was the second loiterer who continued to run west on Water Street after Sullivan had turned up Adelaide Street. Nolan caught up with Lacey at the foot of Waldegrave Street, got a firm grip on him and informed him that he was under arrest. Lacey was luckier than Sullivan and apparently much wiser, for the moment that Nolan had captured him, he identified himself.

Two weeks passed and Kelland reasoned that the secret concerning Sullivan's injury had been well kept for he had heard no member of the force make mention of it. One day Albert Kelland received an order from Sub-Inspector Kenna to appear before Inspector General Carty at 2:00 p.m. which now convinced him that Carty was aware of what had happened to Sullivan. Although Kelland felt under the circumstances he was fully justified in belting Sullivan over the head, one never knew what the outcome of his visit to Carty's office would be. So it was with certain misgivings that he entered into the chief's presence, snapped to attention and saluted. The inspector general did not speak at first, but got up from his chair and began to pace back and forth with his hands behind his back, with Kelland remaining stiffly at attention. Carty crossed back and forth five or six times, then he stopped and facing the constable barked, "At ease!"

"It has come to my notice," said the inspector general, "that you nearly killed Head Constable Sullivan a couple of weeks ago. What have you got to say to that?"

"Well, sir," replied Kelland, "it was probably through God's mercy that I didn't kill him, for I'm afraid that I hit him pretty hard. As far as I could tell, sir, he was a black man reaching for a weapon and knowing that many of those men carry knives, open razors and daggers on their persons, I decided that I had no alternative but to hit him hard enough to knock him out, which I did. I am very sorry for the injury I caused Mr. Sullivan, but what puzzles me is why he did not identify himself to me when I first caught him, as Sergeant Lacey did when Constable Nolan caught him."

"Now, Kelland," said Mr. Carty, "what I am going to say to you must not go any farther than this office. I am not in the habit of criticizing my high ranking officers in the presence of a constable, but what happened to Head Constable Sullivan, he brought on himself. Furthermore, by dressing in disguise and blackening their faces and going forth on the street like that, the head constable and the sergeant were themselves breaking the law. You may go now," finished the inspector general.

A week after the incident here occurred, two members of the night watch, while checking on Water Street, caught two men emerging from a back door of one store, each carrying a brin bag loaded with stolen goods. After being arrested and taken to the police station they made a full confession. They admitted that they were guilty of committing all the breaks and robberies which had taken place. They were convicted and sent to jail for fairly long terms.

Screams After Midnight

V eteran police Sergeant Patrick Whelan was standing by W. J. Murphy's grocery store on Rawlins Cross. The time was two a.m. It was a very calm morning early in October 1936. Rawlins Cross was the usual meeting place for the N.C.O. in charge of the night watch and the two constables who were detailed to patrol the eastern back section of the town.

When Sergeant Whelan was in his late teens he had sailed as a doryman on vessels fishing out of Gloucester, Massachusetts. After that he had served five years in the Royal Navy Reserve prior to joining the police force. I did a lot of police duty with Pat Whelan and I always found him to be a very likeable, enjoyable and courageous companion. He was a born storyteller and when he was relating his experiences while fishing or in the Reserve, it seemed to make the long hours of night watch go much more quickly.

Sergeant Whelan glanced at his watch, it was exactly 2:00 a.m. So he knew that unless something had delayed them, his two men would soon put in an appearance. It was at that moment the screaming started. A woman's screams, very loud and ear splitting. They were long-drawn and sounded horrible. After a few seconds the screams ended with a guttural noise as if the woman emitting them had finally been choked to death. To Whelan it seemed as if the screaming came from the direction of Barnes Road. So he ran in that direction. As he neared Gorman's Lane, he met his two men running towards him.

They told him that they were near the top of Mullock Street when they had heard the screams and it sounded as if they were coming from the direction of Military Road. After a short conference, with all three men agreeing that some woman who had been walking along one of the nearby streets had been viciously attacked and possibly murdered, the three officers split up. With the aid of their flashlights they poked into every lane, backyard, nook and cranny on Barnes Road, Catherine Street, Hayward Avenue, Mullock Street, McDougall Street, Monkstown Road, Military Road and Maxse Street, but found nothing. Of course, Whelan surmised, the woman could have been attacked inside some dwelling. But if she were and the windows and doors in the building had been closed, it would seem impossible for the screaming to sound so loud as it did.

"Anyway," said Whelan, "if some woman has been murdered or just having an oversized nightmare, it is now a matter for the C.I.D. to investigate."

So he went to the Central Fire Hall and telephoned the officer in charge of the C.I.D., District Inspector Edward Whelan, his brother, and informed him of the incident.

"Ok," said Edward, "I'll call in a couple of my men and have them check it out."

The two C.I.D. men assigned to the investigation covered a lot of ground that day and the next. They knocked on more doors than an aspiring M.H.A., questioning dozens of people, but they couldn't find one solitary soul who'd even admit to hearing the screams. They never located any woman who said she had been attacked and they never found the body of a murdered lady either.

Two weeks passed by and no screaming had been reported. At the beginning of the third week, I was the N.C.O. who had been detailed to supervise night watch. I arrived on Rawlins Cross at five minutes to two o'clock Monday morning. It was nearing the end of October, the weather was clear and cold with very little wind. I was standing by W. J. Murphy's grocery store awaiting the arrival of the two constables patrolling that section. The senior of the two was George Lethbridge, his companion was a new member of the force whose name I cannot now recall. I was standing there for about three minutes when the screams started. They came in waves. A woman's screams, high pitched and horrible. Both in the movies and on television I've heard Hollywood actresses emit some pretty soul chilling screams, but none that I've heard from those sources could come anywhere near comparing with the screams I was now hearing.

If it was some lady screaming just for the fun of it or putting on a show for her friends then she was wasting her talent by staying in Newfoundland. For I'm sure that if a Hollywood talent scout had been in the vicinity and heard those magnificent screams he would have endeavoured to locate her and offer her a large sum of money to accompany him to the movie capital and perform her screaming there.

The screaming continued for several seconds then terminated with a guttural sound similar to what Pat Whelan had heard, as if the woman's air supply had been cut off by the pressure of powerful fingers. The screaming sounded to me, also, as if it were coming from the direction of Barnes Road. So I ran that way only to meet Constable Lethbridge and the other man running towards me at a fast clip. My two men, like Sergeant Whelan's men, were certain that the screaming was centred on Miliary Road. So we made a thorough search of the whole area but found nothing.

Acting on my report, members of the C.I.D. again made a thorough investigation, but like the men who haul codtraps and find no fish in them, they made a complete waterhaul. Time marched on and no further reports came in of a lady screaming her head off.

At that time I lived on Barnes Road near the top of McDougall Street. An old lady who lived near me said to me one day, "You fellows are wasting your time looking for that screaming woman. I'd say that you are a hundred years or so too late. For what you heard was the ghost of some poor girl who was murdered by drunken soldiers or some other black-hearted scoundrel a long, long time ago."

Did that old woman have a point? Frankly, I don't know. What puzzled us policemen the most was why some of the residents in the surrounding houses didn't hear those screams which were so loud and ear splitting that even sound sleepers should have heard them.

The Terror of Quidi Vidi Lake

Now every pompous merchant,
And every Lew and Jake,
All jeered there is no terror,
In Quidi Vidi Lake.
Abe Bellman was a schooner man,
He saw the monster first,
When he visited his sister
To quench a little thirst.
He left her house at midnight,
And was walking up the road,
When something blocked his pathway,
That looked like a giant toad.

The night was calm and beautiful,
A full moon, brilliant shone,
You could count the leaves on every tree,
Both large and small, each one,
But an ordinary toad is tiny,
This thing stood fourteen feet,
Its head was easy two yards long,
With eyes as red as meat.
With long clawed toes so rapier-like,
And fiery, fetid breath,
That bayman was no coward,
But he shrank from certain death.

Now as the thing with scaly arms,
Reached out to grasp the man,
He did, no doubt, what I would do,
Just turned about and ran.
And after record running,
He safely reached his craft,
But when he told his story,
His shipmates cried, you're daft.

Yet every little caplin,
Each salmon, trout and hake,
All knew there was a monster,
In Quidi Vidi Lake.

Laughed the mate, that 'shine your sister brews,
It sure must be mighty strong,
To make you see night monsters
That's more than twelve feet long.
Next day the story got about,
While Abe still suffered shock,
And he learned that on the waterfront,
He was the laughing stock.
A girl of sixteen saw it next,
But she would never tell,
For they found her torn body
At the bottom of a well.

And with the doctor's verdict,
There were none who could find flaws,
That the poor girl had been torn apart
By long and mighty claws.
Now every pompous merchant,
Each labourer and fake,
Thought, maybe, there's a monster
In Quidi Vidi Lake.
Then Inspector General Carty,
Sent two constables to guard,
The folks of Quidi Vidi
And patrol each lane and yard.

But at daylight the next morning,
A man stepped through his door,
And found two dead policemen,
Each lying in his gore.
Both mens' skulls were fractured,
And their flesh was ripped and torn,
Though gruesome as this is to tell
Some limbs from them were shorn.

And those who'd heard Abe's story,
And who by much mirth were rent,
Now rose the bayman's stock up to
One hundred, plus percent.

Then the folks in every mansion,
And on every street and flake,
Were frightened of the terror
Of Quidi Vidi Lake.
So, promptly was a meeting held,
And 'twas decided sure, that
One hundred men all armed with guns,
Backed up by a dozen more,
Would surround old Quidi Vidi
And sound the dying knell,
And for all time the village free
Of this monster up from hell.

Then the people got lighthearted,
And the whole place rang with cheers,
As from other places on the coast
Came ready volunteers.
For as the sun was setting,
O'er cliff and meadow green,
Twelve men from Flatrock hove in sight,
With twelve more from Bauline.
And Torbay sent three dozen,
Who were armed with guns and sticks,
From Bay Bulls and Petty Harbour
There showed up twenty-six.

And from the city of St. John's,
There came a hundred more,
Determined that for those three deaths
They'd even up the score.
Now in those times long past and gone,
If disaster vile would feed,
Each neighbour travelled swiftly,
To aid in his neighbour's need.

Then three sarcastic braggarts
Appeared to view the throng,
Sneered they why this brave army
A full two hundred strong?

To slay one little monster,
Ye ought to be ashamed,
But if you're short on courage,
We s'pose ye can't be blamed.
Go home me noble hearties
And sup your old maid's tea,
If this monster need a killin',
It can be done by we.
If yon straight gut a terror,
Might well be slain by three,
My friends will stand on either hand,
And slay the fiend with me.

Two hundred men, indeed, with guns,
Ye must be in your cups,
Then said a Petty Harbour man,
The monster might bring pups.
And if she brings her young along,
The Lord knows how many she's got,
It'll take every gun we got here now
And all the powder and shot.
To put an end to that creature,
If she's as big now as they say,
Yer braggin' and boastin' is a lot of bluff,
So why don't you fade away.

Thus spoke the Petty Harbour man,
And scarcely had he spake,
When from the inky caverns
Of Quidi Vidi Lake,
There rose a slimy monster,
Whose eyes were flashing fire,
So overcome by dread, were some
They grovelled in the mire,

Now our three bogus heros,
Took just one fearful glance,
Then left old Quidi Vidi's shores
So swift, they shed their pants.

They ran so far and fast that night,
And covered so much ground,
No trace of those bold sneersters
Has ever since been found.
And now two hundred muskets,
Were trained upon the fright,
Then acrid smoke and orange flame
Were belched across the night.
And while the grand old village,
Lay buried 'neath that screen,
The blast from all those muzzles,
Was heard in Merasheen.

An asthma-plagued old-timer gasped,
And prayed there'd come a breeze,
For faith, qouth he, this gunshot cure,
Plays hell with my disease.
Now when the smoke had cleared away,
From every lane and house,
All saw the monster still alive,
And playful as a mouse.
And now it turned toward them,
Then straightway climbed the bank,
While the stoutest heart amongst them
Just fluttered and then sank.

And with all hope near vanquished,
They saw the crowd divide,
Then through the ranks two clergymen,
Came on with fearless stride.
Now, the terror, paused right in midstep,
As she eyed the firm approach
Of the Reverend Mr. Hawkins
And the Reverend Father Roach.

While each a cross on high now held,
Toward this monster dank,
It screamed but once, yes screamed and died,
Then toppled down the bank.

And the waters of Quidi Vidi,
Were seen to boil and yaw,
Then the terror quickly vanished
Into their avid maw.
While men and guns against the foe,
Had been of no avail,
It had been demonstrated
That the Holy Cross can't fail.
Some lines ago you may have seen
I thrust all jokes aside,
This tale contains a moral
Whose strength I will not hide.
Perhaps I'm not a Christian man
But this advice I give,
When evil dark enslaves you
Look to the Cross and live.

Crossing the Seas

The above title is deceptive, in that it does not mean crossing the ocean from one point to another, as people who read it may imagine. In this story, "Crossing the Seas" portrays a different meaning altogether.

During the summer of 1904, prices being paid for dried salt cod by the bigger businessmen of the south and southwest coasts of Newfoundland were very low. Back in that day, there was another group who were popularly known as the little merchants. Those men who operated small general stores in various settlements had taken in a considerable amount of fish in trade for foodstuffs and other items. The little merchants in most cases were also codtrap fishermen, so in addition to fish on hand from their trade deals, they all had stored a fairly large bulk as a result of their own fishing operations. In our own town of Lamaline, on the Burin Peninsula, my father owned such a store, situated at the west end of the harbour. John Coady owned one in the east end, James and William Lockyer on the south side and similar stores were operated by Peter Benteau at Lories, eight miles to the west and Thomas Isaacs at Lord's Cove, eight miles to the east.

Visitors arriving from St. John's spread the news around that the fish merchants in the capital were paying higher prices for dried salt cod than were the south coast fish merchants. That story of higher prices prompted the six little men to hold a get together. The outcome of that meeting was that they decided to charter a vessel, load her up with their fish and head for St. John's.

They discovered that the only schooner available to them was a forty ton craft, owned jointly by the brothers James and Thomas Hann, who resided on the south side of Lamaline harbour. This vessel, *Linda Belle*, was rather ancient. She had been engaged at fishing ventures and also at the coasting trade for many, many years. Her hull was pitted and scarred and signs of decay were apparent in certain sections of her bulwarks and deck. James Hann had always sailed in her as captain, while Thomas served as mate or second hand.

When the little merchants approached Captain Hann with a view to hiring his schooner his answer was, "Well, she's old, weary and I guess a little ill, as you fellers knows, she's been laying up for the past two years. But if you wants to take the chance and load her with your fish to voyage to St. John's, I'm willin' to pilot her there."

At this juncture one of the merchants said, "You don't need to take on any crewmen Skipper, for all of us have had sea experience. We can steer, hoist, lower and reef sails. Before we came to you, we agreed that in the event we did hire your schooner we'd be willing to serve under your orders as her crew."

Captain Hann readily went along with that proposal, for he recognized it as a good money saver, which was, obviously, why the merchants had come up with the idea. After a few necessary details were attended to, the *Linda Belle*, was made ready for sea. Then she was loaded to the hatches with the little merchants fish and the trip towards St. John's commenced.

Here they were very fortunate for beautiful sailing weather was experienced all the way along and they arrived in the capital without any incidents worthy of note occurring. Their cargo was discharged and the merchants were more than delighted when they received nearly twice as much money per quintal (one hundred and twelve pounds) from the firm they had dealings with in St. John's than they would have gotten from the fish merchants in their own area. Now having made a fine profit on their fish sales, the men decided to purchase various types of supplies with which to stock their stores for the coming winter. That way, as one of them put it, they could kill two birds with one shot.

So once more the *Linda Belle* was loaded to the hatches, this time with a general cargo. The fine weather was still holding when they left St. John's on August 24, 1904, and Lady Luck continued to smile on them until they neared Placentia Bay. It was necessary for them to cross the mouth of this bay in order for them to reach their home port.

As they steered towards that objective, the wind which had been blowing a smart breeze from the southwest, then died out to a flat calm. The *Linda Belle* started to roll sluggishly in the gentle swells. My father who was at the wheel and Thomas Isaacs on lookout duty up for'ard, noticed that some very dark, ominous looking clouds were piling up over the horizon in the northeast. The other six men were down below in the after cabin. My father called out to Captain Hann to come up on deck. When he got there, my father and Isaacs called his attention to the ugly appearing northeastern sky. The captain eyed those clouds with feelings of misgiving. Old seadog that he was, he knew that they portended trouble.

"Boys," he told the two crewmen, "we're in for a big blow and I predict that it will descend on us in an hour."

The skipper then called all hands up from below and ordered them to double reef the mainsail and foresail, and to batten down the hatches. In the meantime he ordered my father to lash himself to the wheel. Hann then took a stout rope, one end of which he fastened to a stern ringbolt, the other he made fast with clove hitches to the after stay of the main rigging on the starboard side, then he brought it across the deck and secured it to the port side. At this time, his brother Thomas suggested that they should take the mainsail down altogether and tie it up. Whether the skipper was too contrary to go along with his brother's idea or not, he refused to douse the big sail, a mistake which he lived to regret later.

After the sails had been reefed and the hatches battened down securely, the captain ordered the five men he'd called up to go back in the cabin and close it off. He then called Isaacs back and told him to fasten himself to the man rope he'd rigged earlier and Hann himself did likewise. The captain's prophesy regarding the arrival of the storm was near to the minute correct and the precautions he'd taken to meet it most wise, for the August Gale of 1904 was considered to be one of the worst ever to ravage the south coast of Newfoundland and the *Linda Belle* was caught right in the middle of it.

The first squall that struck the schooner pressed on her sails causing her to heel over. Shortly afterwards a much heavier squall boomed along. The power of that wind snapped off the mainboom, just for'ard of the sheet sling. It ripped the ancient mainsail from the boom, gaff and mask racks. Both sails and boom went over the port quarter and disappeared. The end of the boom, still attached to the main sheet, went over the taffrail and was now banging against the vessel's stern. Fearing that it would batter a hole in her side, Captain Hann disengaged himself from the manrope, went aft and severed the sheet with his knife. This caused the rope to run quickly out of the blocks, freeing the boom end which departed astern. The captain and Isaacs were fortunately win'ard of the long section of the boom and sail when they went overside and so escaped possible injury or death.

Freed of the heavy boom and sail, the schooner slowly righted herself. The skipper then shouted an order to my father to throw the wheel down hard and the *Linda Belle* answering her rudder, came up head into the wind. A little later the wheelsman got the old vessel to lay to, which means that her bow was standing a few points away from the teeth of the wind, then by manipulating the wheel he kept her that way.

The next big squall that struck carried away the jumbo, the sail that was set between the foresail and the jib. And the huge wave that followed it plowed the *Linda Belle*'s nose under. But as I heard my father and Tommy Isaacs describe it years later, she appeared to shake herself like a wet dog, then she rose on the next sea. The jib and foresail were nearly new and they held on. The old vessel rode the waves very well for a while, but as the wind increased in violence and the waves reached a greater height, the *Linda Belle*, in sailor's jargon, seemed to be making poor weather of it.

Sea after sea smashed into and over her, so that each time she nosedived, it would seem to the three men that her time had come. Then a wave larger than the ones which had preceded it came in over the vessel's bow and rolled aft. It carried away her dory and engulfed Captain Hann, Isaacs and Father. It tore Isaacs loose from the manrope and deposited him fifteen feet off from the schooner's side. Just as Hann and my father were about to give him up for lost, the backwash of the sea tossed him back against the main rigging. Isaacs grabbed hold of a stay with one hand and managed to keep his grip. Father freed himself from the wheel, went over and seizing Isaacs by the wrist, dragged him back aboard. Miraculously the man was uninjured.

"I'm sure glad that you're still alive Tom," shouted the captain.

"Thanks," Isaacs replied, then calmly added, "this is becomin' a case of wonderin' which is going to win; life or death."

Captain Hann then shouted above the roar of the wind and the sound of lashing spindrift and driving rain, "Boys, she can't last much longer, we must resign ourselves to that."

He'd scarcely uttered those words when the *Linda Belle*'s nose dipped under a big sea, which caused the hardy, courageous Isaacs to yell that she was gone. But Isaacs was wrong for again the old ship shook herself up out of it. But each man knew in his heart that her next nosedive could send her plummeting to the bottom.

Shortly after the last dive, Peter Benteau pushed back the slider over the after cabin companionway and jumped out on deck. He held up his hand and showed it to the three men. It was still light enough for them to see that the Frenchman had a cross painted on the back of that hand. He then turned about and faced the bow of the schooner. As he did so, all hands could discern a huge wave bearing down on the *Linda Belle* with the ferocity of a tiger about to devour a lamb. Peter Benteau held up his cross-marked hand towards the ocean giant. To the amazement of the other three men the big sea flattened out as level as a tennis court and became harmless. Then it dawned on the grey haired skipper that he was a witness to an event which he had often heard about but in all his forty years of roaming the Atlantic had never seen put into practice before.

What the Frenchman had done and what he was still doing is what the title of this story actually means. He was Crossing the Seas. That is how old seamen termed such an action.

When daylight broke on a wild looking ocean, the strength of the wind had lessened considerably. The other crewmen on deck had watched in fascination as the Frenchman adhered devotedly to his faith and continued to Cross the Seas. The crew could observe that the schooner was sailing through a lane of comparatively smooth water while big seas towered up on both her port and starboard sides.

Whereas I do not class myself as much of a Christian, I would like to insert here a verse from an old hymn which I remember being sung many years ago:

Be it the wrath of the storm-tossed sea
Or demons or men or whatever it be
No ocean can swallow the ship where lies
The master of oceans and earth and skies,
They all shall sweetly obey thy will
Peace, peace and be still.

Captain Hann ordered his brother to take command, then he sent a man to relieve my father at the wheel and another to take Isaac's place on the manrope. After which the three, weary, salt encrusted men went below to try and brew a much needed mug of tea. The afternoon was well advanced when the *Linda Belle* sailed proudly and safely into the snug haven of Burin Harbour.

The following day the old vessel was placed on the Burin dry dock. There to the amazement of her crew and the dock workers it was discovered that caulking was nearly loose in some of the seams in her aged bottom. The greatest wonder of all was why the craft didn't spring a leak, for after the schooner came to anchor in Burin her pumps, which were working, had been tried and it was found that she was leaking very little.

Did Crossing the Seas save the *Linda Belle*? Six little merchants and two hardy old seamen were definitely sure of it.

Sea Serpents

I first read the following story when it appeared in Michael Harrington's 'Off Beat History' column of the *Evening Telegram*, dated June 22, 1971. I thought that I should like to add the story to my book for some of the people who read it then may have forgotten all the details. Then again, the people who did not get the opportunity to read it back in 1971 will now be able to peruse it in this volume.

I received a copy of Michael's story from Dr. Bobbi Robertson, the very efficient and cooperative secretary of the Newfoundland Historical Society, and Michael Harrington had kindly given his consent for me to have the story republished here. Michael headlined his story with a question: 'Was it a sea serpent or a giant squid?' Then he goes on and I quote his account verbatim.

'The following story was first related in the St. John's newspapers by Thomas Grant, owner of the schooner *Augusta* of this port, and commanded by Captain Chidley. The incident happened on Saturday, August 11, 1888, somewhere to the south or east of Newfoundland. Two men, James Furlong and Richard Grant were out in their dory setting trawls when they saw a creature moving along in their wake. It was so monstrous an apparition that they threw away their trawls, grabbed their oars and headed for the vessel.

At first they thought they were looking at a school of squidhounds, for they could not believe they were all parts of the same creature, which was rapidly overtaking the dory. When it came close, one of the men seized a bait tub and hurled it at the fish or animal, the head of which, they said, was fifteen to twenty feet out of the water. The monster kept pace with the dory all the way back to the ship. At one point the men said it tried to fling a coil of its tail around the boat, but did not succeed.

After several attempts it fell behind. The dorymen rowed with the strength of horror and despair and their exertions were so great that they tore the skin off their hands. Aboard the schooner the other crew members stared goggle-eyed at the frightening scene. Suddenly, as the dory was about a cable-length from the vessel, the horrifying creature submerged and was seen no more, and all heaved a sigh of relief. Grant and Furlong almost collapsed on reaching the deck.

Here's a description of the denizen of the deep as the men saw it. About twenty feet thick in the middle with a huge fin. Its head was shaped like that of an ugly sculpin, its tail was tapering and resembled the tail of an eel.

After seeing such an apparition, one would think that Captain Chidley would have taken his schooner out of that region of the Grand Banks immediately. But the vessel's trawls had been set out and he didn't want to lose time. So he waited for a couple of hours and when the terrible creature failed to reappear, Chidley ordered his men to leave and pick up the trawls.

Five dories left without incident but as the sixth one left the *Augusta*, the ocean began to boil and bubble and amidst a great swirl of foam the monster again appeared. The men stopped rowing, almost paralysed with fright. And the fearsome creature began to form itself into huge coils as if preparing to attack the dory. One of the men suddenly found his voice and let out a dreadful screech, so loud that it was heard back on board the vessel. Chidley, guessing what had happened, fired a gun as a signal to the other boats that something was wrong and to return at once. The report of the gun also started the men in the sixth dory out of their state of shock and they began to row just in time to miss the devastating stroke of the monster's tail.

Apparently the sea monster was not capable of very great speed, as it could not overtake any of the dories. Every time it reached up or made an attempt to wrap a coil of its body around one of the boats it quickly dropped behind. The men also suspected that its head was its most vulnerable part, as every time its head was raised to look around, it made no direct attack. By this time, Captain Chidley and the other men were ready and Chidley loaded the gun with a second charge and took aim. As the dory neared the schooner and the sea monster raised its head once more, the captain fired. At once the appalling creature sank into the sea, but whether it was hit or not the men could not say.

The men in the sixth dory, the one involved in the second scary chase, were just as upset as their buddies, Grant and Furlong. After they recovered their composure they added more details to the description of the sea serpent's appearance. The first crew, Grant and Furlong, had mainly noted its size. The second crew said the body was brown in colour with stripes across it. Anyway, this was enough for Captain Chidley. He decided to quit the area while he, his men and his ship were still safe and sound. They returned to St. John's where the vessel's owner, Thomas Grant, after hearing their story, gave it to the local papers.

They printed it word for word. Nobody made any attempt to ridicule the men or scoff at their story or even suggest it was pure invention (e.g. a tall story) or a case of a lively imagination. The sceptics, and there were some of course, were somewhat taken aback a couple of weeks later when a newspaper in Gloucester, Massachusetts, the great New England fishing port, published a very similar story. In this case, however, this so-called sea serpent had not been seen far off to sea on the Banks of Newfoundland. This one made its appearance much closer to land in the Bay of Fundy. While

there are not many such stories in our records,' continues
Michael Harrington, 'there is a large number altogether in
the records of various countries. Some of them obviously 'tall
stories,' but there's a large element of truth in others.'

Right here, Michael Harrington offers his own opinion as
to what the dorymen from the banker *Augusta* actually saw.
He states: 'It is reasonable to think, however, that what the
men of the Newfoundland vessel saw in August 1888, was an
oversized giant squid, about which so much has been heard
in recent years. Various points in their account suggest this,
and due allowance must be made for their fear, excitement
and the difficulty of determining if the various coils they saw
belonged to one body or to the many tentacles of a giant
squid. Of course, they could have seen a sea serpent for it is
well known that there are many strange fish in the sea.' With
that observation Michael Harrington ends his story.

I agree with Michael, there are indeed many strange fish
in the sea and some of them have a disturbing habit of
turning up when and where they shouldn't.

Take the case of the coelacanth for example, a fish which
was proclaimed to have been extinct by mighty scientists
since the cretaceous period (noting or pertaining to a period
of the mesozoic era, or from 70 million to 135 million years
ago). But the gentlemen of great learning had their ideas
knocked into a cocked hat when a coelacanth was hauled up
alive and flopping off the coast of southern Africa in 1938.

To return to the dorymen of the banker *Augusta*, those
men, particularly the dory skippers, must have been experi-
enced fishermen and in my opinion, no amount of fear or
excitement would totally dull their powers of observation.
Their very lives, every hour of every day depended on their
observational capabilities. The first dory crew, Grant and
Furlong, described the monster as being eighty to one hun-
dred feet long, about twenty feet thick in the middle with a
huge fin. Its head was like that of an ugly sculpin, the tapering

tail resembling that of an eel. They also stated that the serpent raised its head fifteen to twenty feet out of the water. According to those details given by them, I would say that their powers of observation were working at a high level.

The second dory crew observed that the monster's body was brown with stripes across it. You will see, I'm sure, that the second crew did not do too badly either when they noticed those markings. That description, 'brown in colour with stripes across it,' matches exactly with accounts of sea serpents I have read of that made appearances in other areas of the globe, wherein eye witnesses have noticed the brown colour and the stripes. Then the second dory crew began to row just in time to miss a devastating stroke of the monster's tail. Sometime during the 1870s a boat occupied by two brothers and the son of one of them, was crossing the tickle between Portugal Cove and Bell Island when a giant squid surfaced near the boat. It snaked a tentacle inboard, wrapping it around the boy's father. The other man panicked at the awesome sight and became helpless, but the boy kept his head and seizing an axe, he very bravely attacked the big squid, chopping off the tentacle, thereby freeing his father from certain death. After its tentacle was severed, the monster disappeared and wasn't seen again.

So now I would like to express another opinion, which is, if it had been a giant squid that pursued the dorymen from the *Augusta*, it would not have fooled around raising up its head so often, nor slashing about a tentacle that the men might have mistaken for a tail. No, a giant squid would have slipped a tentacle in over the dory's gunnel, wrapped it around the bodies of the fishermen and dragged them to their doom. Furthermore, if the creature had been a giant squid, there would have been no ugly, sculpin type head with a neck that stretched several feet above the water. There would have been no hundred foot length, no eel-like tail and certainly no stripes across the body.

Near the end of his narrative, Michael stated that following the Newfoundland dorymen's experience, a sea serpent made an appearance in the Bay of Fundy. This caused me to wonder if I could get more information on that sighting. So I wrote some letters, directing them to points in Massachusetts. As a result I received three separate responses dealing with the subject. A Mr. Victor Clarke, a former Newfoundlander, now residing in Gloucester, forwarded me copies of newspaper clippings listing some sea serpent sightings.

The second answer to my enquiries came from a Mr. and Mrs. J. R. LaFond of East Gloucester, Massachusetts, who enclosed newspaper clippings which told stories of sea monsters which had been sighted by several fishermen and others off the coasts of New England. The LaFonds also sent along a sketch of a fearsome looking creature which portrays it as it was described by fishermen who saw it off Cape Ann during 1981 and 1982.

Dr. William Hoyt, a resident of Rockport, Massachusetts, sent along a short article, evidently copied from some newspaper, which described a sea serpent that was seen by a scientist in Gloucester harbour in 1817. The man who saw it said the creature's head was like the head of a turtle and stuck up out of the water. There were three lumps on the back of the neck that extended about ten inches above the surface. Also enclosed was a sketch of the serpent, showing the three lumps, but whether this drawing was the work of the scientist who saw the creature or from some other person's pen, nobody knows today.

Dr. Hoyt told me that he found the account of the sighting of a sea monster in a newspaper dated September 7, 1888, that could have been the same animal which Michael Harrington made reference to in his story. The newspaper states that the veracity of the three young men involved in the incident was vouched for by the *Daily News* (American paper). It seems that the three, truthful, young men were out in a dory near the outer can buoy (location not given) when their attention was directed to something in the water about twenty feet away. They swore that it was not a whale. They were equally sure of that, for one of them had seen whales and knew of their length and appearance. The fish, or whatever it may be called, was larger than a whale. Its head was as large as a barrel and it had eyes of unusual proportions. A fin-like back showed itself in places out of the water. It floated very lazily near the dory, then with a flap of its long tail went down, but reappeared again much farther away, then went down and was seen no more.

Dr. Hoyt, who is a scientist, also stated that a Mr. J. M. Allen of Hartford, Connecticut, reported in an issue dated August 3, 1888, that twenty-four appearances of a similar animal were observed during the past forty years, nine since 1860 and five since 1875. The areas mentioned were the coasts of Greenland, Norway, Nova Scotia and Massachusetts, off the Hebrides, off Sicily and New Guinea, in the Indian Ocean, and in the South Atlantic between the Cape of Good Hope and St. Helena.

According to those reports, if our dorymen from the banker *Augusta* were just seeing things or permitting their imaginations to run riot, then they weren't the only ones to do so.

A Sea Mystery Solved

She sailed when sunshine lit the seas,
And over her deck blew a spanking breeze,
Just the wind to fill her sails,
She appeared alive, this schooner new,
In the best of spirits seemed her crew
As they waved good-bye from her rails.

But she never reached that northern bay,
Wherein her destination lay,
Nor was she seen again,
The coastal boats searched far and wide,
While airplanes hovered o'er the tide
And sought her, but in vain.

I was twelve years old when that occurred,
And ten years had not my memory blurred,
For my brother was her mate,
I remembered the vessel, I remember him,
Neither time nor space could ever dim
The mystery of their fate.

I now had joined the R.C.N.,
And was on a corvette called the *Wren*,
The moon rode full and clear,
When we were cruising off the shore
I'd say five miles or maybe more,
Magnetic, from Cape Spear.

Now I was in the watch on deck,
When far astern just a speck
Appeared a spot of white.
And then it grew and broadened fast,
My fingers dug into the mast,
As I saw a ghostly sight.

'Twas a schooner, she was glistening white,
And all her crew on deck looked light
And transparent, off our stern.
'Twas then I gasped, for no mistake,
That craft there, sailing in our wake
Was the schooner that didn't return.

And then she came abreast our beam,
So close was she I could count each seam
In the planks, o'er her shapely frame,
She raced our corvette neck and neck,
And from her bows rolled a bloody fleck,
It was then I could read her name.

And that figure, standing by the bell,
It was my brother, I could easy tell
My brother who was her mate.
I tried to hail him, but no sound would come
For, I seemed to be paralyzed and dumb,
My tongue would not rotate.

Then the vessel shook from stern to stem,
While foam encircled her like a hem,
And she heeled over, as if in careen,
It was then I beheld her, as plain as day
Not more than eighty feet away,
A ghostly submarine.

And then the shells from her deck gun struck,
They riddled the schooner from keel to truck,
And her hull burst out in flames.
As her crew leaped from the stricken craft
The enemy sailors fore and aft, shot them,
More cruel than Jesse James.

And now my numb limbs came alive,
Then I made what some folks call a dive,
To the corvette's for'ard gun.
I fired a shell at the submarine,
For I felt that I had a righteous spleen
Against that murderous Hun.

And then the officer of the watch
He lifted me up by neck and crotch,
Yelling, "You're crazier than a bat!
Without an order you fired that gun
Just what in heaven's name, my son,
Did you think you were shooting at?"

"You mean, sir," I shouted, "you did not see,
Out there on the ocean? That vicious melee?"
"I did not," he sternly said.
Then all the sailors who were gathered around
Winked and whispered, then most profound,
Said, poor Kelly's gone off his head.

I told him the story, but not without dread,
"I believe that you're telling the truth," he said.
"For your record here has been clean.
And now, if what I think is right,
Tonight you were granted second sight,
For you saw things we had not seen.

"I've been told that at times the Lord breaks seals,
On some of his mysteries and often reveals
Things to persons who are concerned,
It must be true, for now you know
What happened to your brother so long ago,
For sure, that much you have learned.

"Yes boy!" he mused, "it's clear to me
That you were given the right to see
How murder was done off this coast,
And you know, sometime submarine too,
She must have met her Waterloo,
For, she likewise appeared as a ghost."

Then to the ocean I turned my eyes,
And opened them wide in great surprise,
For nothing was in sight.
Marauder and schooner had faded away,
And the moonlight there as bright as day
Showed naught but us and the night.

What Happened to Captain Rideout

In the fall of 1874, the brigantine, *Flirt*, under the command of Captain Fredrick Rideout, set sail from St. John's. The vessel was bound to Bay of Islands for the purpose of picking up a cargo of herring. The *Flirt* had been chartered by the firm of William Frew who conducted a business on Water Street. A brigantine is a two masted vessel which is square-rigged on the foremast and fore and aft rigged on the mainmast, with three or four, usually four, jib type sails set between the two masts.

The *Flirt*, in all probability, was built in England as so many vessels of her type owned in Newfoundland had their origin in the Old Country. The *Flirt* was put up for sale in January 1870. Her measurements listed on the For Sale sign read: length, 104 feet 30-10ths.; breadth, 24 feet 10-10ths.; depth, 12 feet 70-10ths.; gross tons, 167. Interested parties were invited to apply to James and William Boyd, St. John's. No mention was made as to whether the Boyds were her owners or if they were acting as sales agents for her owners. Later I will refer to the man who owned her at the time she started the voyage to Bay of Islands.

In addition to his regular crew of eight, which included the captain and the cook, Rideout took along thirteen additional men, twelve of these were coopers, the thirteenth was a regular carpenter. Twenty-one men in all. The *Flirt*'s measurements point out the fact that she was a pretty husky vessel for that day and age. As the captain and mate or second hand usually slept in the after cabin, it meant that there was ample room in her fo'c's'le to accommodate the remaining nineteen

men. With so much space up for'ard, it suggests to me that at
one time the *Flirt* may have been used as a Banks fisherman.

The season for securing herring was well advanced when
Rideout left St. John's, so it can be surmised that both the
captain's and the Frew firm's reason for carrying so many
coopers was to speed up the work of salting the herring and
heading up the barrels which contained the fish, for if they
delayed too long, the waters of Bay of Islands may freeze over
quickly and the *Flirt* could be trapped there until spring. On
many occasions in the past, Newfoundland, American and
Canadian schooners on likewise missions had been caught by
an early freeze up and were forced to remain solidly jammed
until the ice melted as the warmer season advanced.

Fate decreed, however, that Captain Rideout would
never load the *Flirt* with herring. Before he came to the
entrance of Bay of Islands, a violent wind storm descended on
his vessel and she was driven ashore at a place called Wild
Cove, which is situated on the opposite side of the peninsula
that forms the outer section of the bay. At that time the area
around Wild Cove was and possibly still is completely made
up of sand. Consequently, with the action of the wind and
waves, the *Flirt* soon became embedded. She eventually
heeled over on her beam ends listing inward towards the
land.

Certain conditions and equipment from the vessel which
had been observed by the sixth officer sent to investigate the
disappearance of the *Flirt*'s crew, indicated plainly to him
that all hands had landed safely from the stricken craft.

Then it is logical to imagine that Rideout and his men
would have been forced to abandon the schooner for two
main reasons. First, it would have been impossible to live on
board owing to her heavy list. Secondly, there would be the
fear that, with a high spring tide coupled with an offshore
wind, she may slip off into deep water and sink, as no doubt

her bottom seams would have opened up somewhat while big seas were pounding her and grinding her on the sand.

Three years passed away, then rumours began to drift into St. John's, ugly rumours, about the fate of Rideout and his crew. They had been murdered to a man, one report stated. And the finger of suspicion pointed toward three brothers named Benoit: Gil, Exavior and Francois, who resided in Benoit's Cove. One account asserted that the Benoits lived in an isolated spot on the Port-Au-Port Peninsula, but such was not the case. As the second last policeman to conduct an investigation regarding the supposed murders disclosed, they lived in Benoit's Cove, Bay of Islands, not too far from Curling.

The newspapers of that day seized upon the rumours like hungry wolves and printed what was later reputed to be the wildest kind of lies and slander about the Benoit brothers. Some of them also demanded that the Benoits be tried for murder. Those embellished stories, together with cries for action by the relations of the missing seamen, eventually stirred the authorities to have an investigation made.

The general story constructed by the press went as follows. Following the shipwreck, Captain Rideout and his men after getting ashore, engaged the Benoits to guide them to where they could locate a vessel. Then, while travelling to the place designated by the brothers, the suspects shot to death the whole crew, robbed them and afterwards chopped a hole in the ice, then stuffed the bodies in.

Now where Rideout's vessel grounded, there lived an old man named Jocko. Another rumour had it that the Benoits fearing Jocko would inform people that the shipwrecked men had gone off with them to try and find a vessel, had returned to the old man's tilt and bought his silence with some of the stolen money.

When the heads of government in St. John's decided to investigate, they selected Captain Erskine of the H.M.S.

Eclipse to do the job. To me, selecting the captain of a British
warship to investigate a case of possible mass murder seems
rather peculiar, in view of the fact there was available at that
time Inspector General Carty. As I outlined in a previous
chapter, Inspector Carty had served for many years in the
Royal Ulster Constabulary and was a commissioned officer
on that force before coming to Newfoundland. In addition to
being an experienced policeman himself, Carty brought
along with him a number of other men who had served a long
period of time on the police force of Northern Ireland. For
example, there was Head Constable O'Brien, Sergeant
Coughlan, Constable O'Farrell and others. Later, Carty at-
tached to our force two more former members of wide
experience in the Ulster Constabulary. They were Head
Constable McCowan and Head Constable Doyle. With all
those top-notched police officers on hand, I find it difficult to
understand why the government came up with Captain Er-
skine to lead the investigation.

Captain Erskine's instructions were to proceed to the
west coast, probe into the case and make arrests if necessary.
Later, Judge Lilly of the Supreme Court went out there to add
his skills to the inquiry. The presence of a Justice of the
Supreme Court involved in the investigation also gives me
cause for wonderment. For during my nineteen years as a
member of the Newfoundland Constabulary I never knew or
heard of any judge or magistrate investigating an alleged
crime. I have known Supreme Court judges and magistrates
to visit scenes of crimes, but then only after the police had
investigated and the suspects stood before them at the bar
charged with a criminal act. But back in the 1870s, one never
knows what might have prompted Judge Lilly to take an
active part. Of course, he could have been ordered to do so
by the Minister of Justice.

It was during the summer of 1877 that Captain Erskine
set out to solve the mystery of the disappearance of Captain

Rideout and his crew. Whether Inspector General Carty felt slighted at having Captain Erskine go over his head in this matter, or whether he actually received instructions from the Minister of Justice or otherwise, the police chief went to the west coast anyway and conducted his own investigation. Carty arrived there accompanied by two policemen and interrogated a number of people including old Jocko, but if that old gentleman knew anything about the murder of Captain Rideout and his crew, he told the police chief and his men nothing.

One other rumour which had been going the rounds for some time was that the Benoits had been making a business of murdering and robbing seamen. A remark passed later by the mother of the suspects seemed to bear out the fact that this rumour was not entirely false. But I will go into that later.

To come back to Captain Erskine, he must have thought he'd unearthed a bit of substantial evidence against the Benoits, for he arrested all three brothers and lodged them in jail in Channel. Later the prisoners were escorted to His Majesty's Penitentiary in St. John's. During their incarceration, Francois, the youngest of the trio, died. Some people declared that the young man died from anguish and despair as a result of the supposed injustice which had been inflicted upon him. After the death of Francois, his two elder brothers were released from custody as the crown had failed to secure sufficient evidence to bring them to trial.

Now, it seems that some of the newspapers who at first desired to see the Benoits doing their final dance at the end of a rope for the murder of the Rideout crew, were suddenly gushing with sympathy for them. Here's how one St. John's paper put it: The poor Benoits are again at liberty, but they are no longer three, sorrow has done its work. Let us hope that they shall at least meet where the injustice and folly of prudes have no dominion.

Then members of the public got into the act. Letters to

the editors' columns roasted the press unmercifully for the manner in which they handled the Benoit case. Captain Erskine, Judge Lilly and Inspector General Carty also came under fire. 'No one,' asserted a letter writer, 'can exonerate Captain Erskine who had arrested these poor fellows, subjecting them to hardships that could be harsh were they even condemned by a jury of their peers. Captain Erskine should have realized that there were no grounds for arrest. Who is to blame for the death of young Benoit? The circumstances of his death are plainly put by Dr. Howley, who shows conclusively, that it was in consequence of his unjust arrest that he came to his untimely end. He was born and bred a British subject,' the writer went on, 'Had he not so good a right to have the cause of his death scrutinized as that of the Rideouts themselves?'

Other sympathetic letters appeared in the press and sympathy was all that the surviving Benoits received. But were the Benoit brothers as innocent as their sympathizers would have people believe? Personally, I will not express an opinion regarding the question. I prefer to leave it to the reader to pass his or her own judgement when the conclusion of the Rideout/Benoit story arrives.

Even before Captain Erskine commenced his investigation, the government had been disturbed over reports which seeped into St. John's regularly concerning acts of lawlessness that were being committed in the Bay of Islands area. Some of those reports were not founded entirely on rumour, for the Minister of Justice had received numerous letters from concerned citizens outlining in detail what was taking place there in the nature of drunk and disorderly conduct, assaults on people, citizens being held up and robbed even in broad daylight. Each fall a large fleet of schooners would arrive in Bay of Islands to load herring cargoes. According to my late friend Gordon Thomas of Gloucester and Ipswich, one fall no less than fifty-four American vessels were anchored at the same time off Curling. Then, of course, there would have been the smaller fleets from Newfoundland and Nova Scotia anchored there as well. Consequently there had to be times when dozens of crewmen from those schooners would be on the loose roaming around Curling and Petrie's Crossing. Half fill the men with liquor and it spelled trouble. When I was stationed in Corner Brook in the 1920s as a member of the Newfoundland Constabulary, an old man who had lived in Curling back in the 1870s and 80s, told me in those days you could say that every third hose was a public house. So according to his statement, liquor was readily available. There were laws on the statute books to cover such breaches of the law I mentioned, but no person was there who possessed the authority to enforce them, i.e. police or magistrates.

Later, more letters coming into the government during 1876 and 1877 were not simply requesting the law's protection, they were demanding it. So the premier called a cabinet meeting where the complaining, demanding letters from Bay of Islands were perused minutely. After which the decision was made to send a magistrate and a member of the Terra Nova Constabulary to the area, with the hoping that they would make a serious effort to establish law and order there.

Apparently, the government of the day had succumbed to the same weakness that some of our latter day governments are suffering from, because they reasoned that they would be unable to locate a man in Newfoundland capable of holding down the post of magistrate in Bay of Islands. Import a foreign expert, they decided, that's what they needed, a real tough character who would not tolerate any shenanigans from law breakers. So they wrote the British government, giving them the lowdown on their Bay of Islands problem and requested that the mighty ones beyond the seas select and send them a man able enough to handle the vexing situation.

As it turned out, they secured the services of a real dandy, in the person of William Howorth, the retired commander of a British man-o-war. When Commander Howorth arrived in St. John's, he became the guest of His Excellency, the Governor, and enjoyed the comforts of Government House. It appears that Mr. Howorth was not the type of man to spend too much time fooling around, for after he'd rested a couple of days, he sent a note to Inspector General Carty requesting him to choose one of his constables to accompany him to Bay of Islands.

"I will need a good man," he told the police head. Then added, "Kindly instruct the policeman of your choice to report to me at Government House."

My father, Constable Edgar Kelland, was the man whom Carty selected to accompany the new magistrate. The Inspector General then dashed off a note which he addressed to Commander Howorth, ordering my father to deliver it to him personally, when he arrived at Government House.

When Howorth read Carty's note, he laughed out loud. Carty had written, 'Commander, you asked me to send you a good man. I would like to inform you sir, that I have none but good men to send.'

Mr. Howorth talked with and questioned my father for upwards of an hour, then told him that he would do alright. He instructed the constable to report back to Mr. Carty. The commander handed him a note addressed to the police chief which evidently informed him that Constable Kelland would accompany the new magistrate to Bay of Islands, for Carty passed him his order of transfer immediately.

Before father had left Government House, Mr. Howorth told him to stand by at police headquarters and await further orders. In the meantime, the Minister of Justice had administered the oath of office and allegiance to Commander Howorth, making his appointment as a magistrate official. While the transfer order and the oath of allegiance were being administered, an item in the newspaper, *Newfoundlan-*

der, appeared to adequately lend support to the complaints received from concerned citizens of Bay of Islands. It read: The Bay of Islands area, for some time, has been the refuge of outlaws, who seem to have considered themselves beyond the reach of the law.

Three days after their appointments had been in effect, the magistrate and the constable left St. John's for Bay of Islands. They took passage on the steamer *Hercules*, which was in service all along the west coast.

Now while all this was going on, the relatives of Captain Rideout and his crewmen were raising a storm with the government generally and with the Department of Justice in particular. They demanded that a further investigation be made regarding the disappearance of their loved ones. They could hardly be blamed for making such demands as three years had gone by since the *Flirt* left St. John's and no word had been received from any member of her crew during all that time. Now, the relatives insisted that if another investigation disclosed the fact that their men had indeed been murdered, they earnestly requested that everything be done to bring the murderer or murderers to justice. Before my father departed for his new station, Inspector General Carty called him into his office and informed him of the demands being made by the relatives of the missing men. Then he instructed him that after his arrival at Curling and as soon as conveniently possible, that he was to reopen the Rideout case. Carty further advised him that before an enquiry could be started, he must consult with Commander Howorth and gain his approval for the venture.

At the first opportunity that presented itself, my father, in accordance with instruction from Inspector Carty and with the blessing of Magistrate Howorth, reopened the investigation. He first made an early morning walk to Benoit's Cove, where he came upon the two Benoit brothers. They were working near their shack cutting up firewood. He knew them by sight having seen them in the court room in St. John's. He talked with them for a while, but did not mention Captain Rideout. He felt that it wouldn't have done any good for him to do so. While father was talking with the brothers, he noticed a girl whom he judged to be thirteen to fourteen years old, sitting near the woodpile, crooning to a rag doll which she held in her arms. She paid not the slightest attention to the policeman. She acted as if she didn't even see him. As the snug fitting police uniform with its broad, leather waist belt and the head covering of a spiked helmet, was an entirely new mode of dress even to most adults in the locality, and was the cause of much interest on the part of men, women and children, the girl's lack of curiosity puzzled him. He asked the elder brother, Gil, if she was his daughter.

"Yeah," replied Gil. Then he tapped his forehead and announced, "She is crazy, that one. Her mother is dead and my mother who keeps house for us takes care of her."

My father had a special interest in the investigation, for the very good reason that one of his first cousins was a member of the Rideout crew. Leaving the Benoits, he travelled on. He did not imagine that he would experience too much difficulty in locating Wild Cove, as the area had been described to him by some men of Curling. They told him it would be hard to miss, as most of the wrecked brigantine *Flirt* was still there. Before he reached Wild Cove, he noticed an old tilt standing just off the trail. Thinking that the owner was somewhere in the nearby woods he called out several times but received no answer. He surmised that the tilt was the residence of the old man, Jocko. He later learned that Jocko had disappeared about a month before the arrival of the magistrate and policeman at Curling and no one seemed to know of his whereabouts.

On reaching Wild Cove, my father observed that the vessel had been driven well above the normal highwater mark. Her masts, booms and gaffs were missing. All the planks together with the bulwarks were gone from her seaward side. Most of the timbers on that side had also disappeared. Her entire fore deck had fallen in. As there was no evidence to show that her masts had snapped off, he concluded that they had been salvaged by some men building a new schooner. This type of salvage operation had been common in the past wherein schooner builders had welcomed getting readymade spars from some wreck that would save them an awful lot of work in manufacturing new ones from virgin sticks. He guessed also, that the booms, gaffs and yards had been taken along with the masts. He stepped upon the vessel's rail but did not land on the after or break deck which appeared to be in fair condition, as it was all too obvious that seagulls had been using the wreck as a resting place during the three years which followed her grounding. It was a mess. Had the *Flirt* been stranded on a rocky shore there is no doubt but that she would have been reduced to splinters long since.

As my father walked away from the wreck he noticed that a stand of fairly thick lumber was growing all along the shoreline, then there was a clear space and more timber was in evidence on the low rise at the back of it. Then he saw some of the vessel's sails lying around partly buried in the sand. They were green with mould and mildew. Next he saw where a rough table had been constructed of two by fours and planks, but it was in a state of collapse, near it was the remains of a large fireplace. On examining the sails he identified the schooner's mainsail and other sails. My father had been going to sea for six years prior to his joining the Constabulary and had been shipwrecked no less than three times. So he reasoned that he could form a very good idea of what had occurred after the *Flirt* had become solidly grounded.

Captain Rideout and his men would have come ashore because of the conditions mentioned previously. Then possibly after the storm had abated and the tide had gone down, they returned to the ship and brought ashore foodstuffs, bedding, tools and other necessary items. When father pulled aside the sails, underneath he'd discovered the poles over which they had been draped to form tents.

He found there also, blankets, cooking utensils, two saws, four hatchets, three shovels and various other types of carpenter's and cooper's tools, in addition there was an old musket. All these items were caked with rust. There was also a few coils of rope. It was first reported that Rideout and his men after landing had lived in a tilt. There was no tilt, nor any evidence that one had ever existed. In any case it would have taken quite an oversized tilt to accommodate twenty-one men. No, it was plain that they'd slept in their two, large, makeshift tents. It was obvious too, that the cook performed most of his duties outdoors, that is if weather conditions permitted. The men had taken their meals around the table which my father had found collapsed. If the weather became unsuitable, of course, they could eat in their tents. My father also noticed that the table had been set up close to the woods that grew along by the shore, a sheltered location against inshore winds. It appeared that Captain Rideout decided to remain in the vicinity of his wrecked vessel for a while, probably in the hope that some craft would happen along and rescue them.

My father entered the woods, as he thought he might find some clue there which would aid him in solving the case. He found nothing. As he was about to step out of the timber again, he felt a tug on the tail of his tunic. Turning about quickly, he was amazed to discover the Benoit girl standing behind him. He hadn't heard her approach.

She said, "My name is Agnes. I want to tell you I am not crazy, like my father tell you. I act like this all the time to fool my father and uncle. My grandmother, she knows I'm not crazy. You see, my grandmother and me, we do not like many of the things my father and uncle do."

"What do you mean by that?" father asked.

"Well," she replied, "I will tell you a story and it will be the truth. After you left our shack, my father and my uncle took their guns and went into the country. I know they will be gone for a couple of days because they are huntin' deer (caribou). That is why I follow you here. Now I will tell you. One day my father and my uncle come home and hung their long guns on the rack in the kitchen. My grandmother and me, we noticed that the clothes and boots of both of 'em was covered wit blood. My grandmother, she say, 'Gil, Exavior, where you get all that blood on you?' My father say that they killed some gulls on the Wild Cove Point. But my grandmother say, 'No gulls you kill, you kill more poor men now. You kill more poor men now.' "

It was obvious from that remark that the old lady must have been aware that her sons had killed men previously. It also tied in with the rumour mentioned earlier, to the effect that the Benoit brothers had made a business of murdering and robbing seamen.

"Well," continued the girl, "when my grandmother say that, my father got mad and told her to shut up and mind her own business. then the two of them went into their bedroom and shut the door. I then leaved the kitchen and creeped around to the back wall of their room. There is a crack in that wall and I peeped through it and saw my father take off his mackinaw, around his middle was a piece of fishin' line and hangin' down from that line was a canvas bag. He untie this bag and upsot it on the bed. It was full of gold. I seen my father make two piles of this gold. He give my uncle one and he took the udder, then they stow the gold away in their pockets. I run round to front now and was singin' to my doll when they come out.

"They had their guns with 'em and they start to walk down the path towards Wild Cove. After a bit I foller 'em. I keep to the bushes all the way, so they do not see me. Bom by (by and by) they come to where the big ship is. They lay down their guns, then my father take a shovel and my uncle, he take a shovel and they dig in the sand. Pretty soon they haul up the bodies of two poor mans, they keep diggin' until they root up twenty poor mans."

Here the policeman interrupted her to ask, "Are you sure there was not twenty-one men?"

Agnes replied, "I is sure. I can count real good. I count 'em three and four times, they was exactly twenty mans." Then she said, "When all the mans had been digged up, they make away with 'em, one after the udder. My father, he take the heads and my uncle, he take the foots and carry 'em to a deep, muddy pond just in back there," she pointed to the woods. "And then they trow 'em in. Then they pick up their guns and walk for home. And me," she smiled, "I run back in the country apiece, then I take a shortcut and I get back home ahead of 'em."

Now my father asked her, "What would happen if your father and your uncle caught you spying on them?"

"Oh," she replied readily, "they would kill me right away."

"Did the men who came here before, the judge and the policeman, ask you or your grandmother any questions?"

"No, they come and take my father and my two uncles away, but they did not speak to us or even look at us."

It was common knowledge around St. John's that Captain Rideout had in his possession when he left the capital a canvas bag full of gold. The accountant at Frew's released the information that he'd counted out a sufficient amount of gold to enable Captain Rideout to purchase the herring and pay off his men. The gold he had placed in a canvas bag. Was Gil Benoit's daughter telling the truth? The canvas bag of gold which she stated was in her father's possession seemed to indicate that she was.

As she finished her story, Agnes glanced up at the sky, then said, "I will go now or it will be dark before I get home."

She started off at a fast run and quickly disappeared into the woods on the opposite side of the open space. My father kept on searching for clues until he realized that darkness was approaching. As he had no desire to be on that path after nightfall, he walked back to the old tilt and spent the night there. As daylight broke he left and travelled to Curling.

That afternoon, he obtained a search warrant from Magistrate Howorth which would legally permit him to make a search of the Benoit premises. He also gave his Honour all the details pertaining to the activities of the Benoit brothers at Wild Cove as had been related to him by Agnes. In the meantime, he described to the magistrate conditions as he had found them near the wreck.

Early the next morning he hired two men with pickaxes and shovels, then they walked to Benoit's Cove. When they reached the cabin, he instructed the men to dig around the most likely looking places, especially if they noticed any spot where the ground appeared to have been recently disturbed. He told them also that if they unearthed any items that may have come from Rideout's vessel or from any of her crew, to notify him immediately. On entering the shack, he showed the warrant to Mrs. Benoit and explained its significance. She simply shrugged her shoulders and made no objection to the search. But a complete ransacking of the shack turned up absolutely nothing. He knew that if he did find gold coins it would have been impossible for anyone, including the accountant at Frew's, to identify them as having come from the sack which Captain Rideout carried because those coins were not specifically carrying identifying marks and all coins apart from the various sizes and denominations look alike. Furthermore, he learned from the two men who accompanied him to Benoit's Cove that the suspects from time to time worked at loading herring on vessels, including those of the

Newfoundland fleet, and in the 1870s men were nearly always paid in gold. What he actually hoped to find was the canvas bag or some item from the vessel that had belonged to a crew member which could be definitely identified by a relative and could bring about the conviction of the Benoits.

As he emerged from the shack, the Benoits returned from their hunting trip. They did not appear in the least put out that a policeman and two other men were searching their premises. My father told them point blank that they had been searching for gold or any other article that may have come from the *Flirt*.

Gil replied very calmly, "You are wasting your time here, because we took nothing from Captain Rideout, his vessel or his men. We never even seen 'em."

So father and his two men were obliged to return to Curling empty-handed.

My father had been thinking hard about Agnes Benoit's story. As a result, he formed the opinion that Rideout had never gotten the chance to leave Wild Cove. After the shipwreck, a rumour began circulating that Rideout had hired the Benoits to guide him to Port-Au-Port. When that story surfaced, somebody familiar with the area pointed out that the idea was silly, owing to the great distance he would be obliged to travel. My father thought that such a great trek on Rideout's part would be utterly ridiculous, for the distance from Wild Cove to Port-Au-Port was, as the crow flies, over forty miles. The distance from Wild Cove to Curling was only half the distance, which would be over a well worn path, not too hard to follow. Whereas on the journey to Port-Au-Port, the men would be obliged to cross brooks, bogs and to have to often force their way through timber.

To view the situation rationally, here was Captain Rideout a master mariner for several years. Surely he would have had on board his ship, charts of the entire bay to which he was travelling. All the settlements from the bay's entrance to the mouth of the Humber River would appear on those charts. Even in the 1870s, Curling was a fairly large settlement. Near Curling were the smaller villages of Petrie's Crossing, Corner Brook and Humbermouth. Common sense should declare that once Captain Rideout despaired of getting help from the sea, he and his men would walk to one of the settlements mentioned until they could secure passage home and the captain had the money to pay for accommodation. Anyway, that is the conclusion my father came to.

He then decided to return to Wild Cove. Arriving there, he made a thorough examination of the table the men had used. Cleaning the sand and dirt off the top side of the board he observed grooves running the length of it, on both sides. Right then he figured that he could deduce what had occurred at that spot three years earlier.

He thought that for two or three men to shoot and kill twenty-one men outright under ordinary circumstances would be an almost impossible task. The guns in those days were muzzle loaders; consequently, after they had been fired, they would need to be reloaded before they could be used again. He considered that the entire crew would not have been bunched together at any one time unless a special function was being observed. So if the murderers fired on them while they were standing in loose formation, the largest number they could hope to wound or kill would be half a dozen men. Once fired, of course, the guns would be useless, except as clubs. It is hardly likely that the fifteen survivors would give the killers time to reload or permit themselves to be clubbed to death with the back stocks of the muzzle loaders in the hands of two or three men.

No, the murderers had to come up with a better idea if their vicious intentions were to be successful. An idea that had to be studied with patient assiduity, which must enable the killers to knock all hands down simultaneously. My father reasoned that after the vessel had become hopelessly

grounded and the crew had managed to land, their move-
ments were closely watched by persons hidden in the woods.
Assuming that those characters had been the Benoits, they
would have been fully aware that the captain of the *Flirt* would
be carrying a large amount of money to purchase a cargo of
herring. So they would remain concealed until a favourable
opportunity presented itself.

That moment came when all twenty-one men were seated
at the table to partake a meal. Now with the entire crew
seated, ten on one side of the table and eleven on the other,
it would have been easy for the killers to creep through the
woods until they were within gunshot of that table. Still
assuming that it was the Benoits, my father knew that those
men were half Indian and they'd been stalking game since
they were small boys; consequently, they would have the skill
to reach the desired distance without making a sound or
being seen. Agnes Benoit had crept upon my father noise-
lessly in thick woods, he'd never even heard the rattle of a
leaf.

Here I would like to state that Agnes Benoit never impli-
cated the third brother, the youngest, Francois, in the telling
of her story. My father questioned her about him, but she
answered that he was not present when Gil and Exavior came
home covered in blood, neither was he there when the other
two dug up the bodies and disposed of them. So it is quite
possible that the young man was quite innocent of any evil
doing and was wrongfully arrested. As some of the letter
writers had suggested, he might have died from anguish and
despair over the injustice imposed on him.

When the crew was seated and commenced to eat, the
killers, their long guns loaded with buckshot, took aim at
them. Gil covering one side of the table, Exavior the other.
Then both gunmen fired together, with the heavy buckshot
drilling through the two lines of men, wreaking terrible,
bloody havoc. One buckshot, for example, if it enters a vital

spot in the human body, is capable of causing death and perhaps a disabling wound if it strikes some other region. So what men were not killed outright in the blasts, the brothers could have easily finished off with the butts of their guns as they lay wounded and helpless on the ground. The grooves along the table too were obviously made by some of the buckshot, while other pellets did their deadly work.

I would like to add that my father had absolutely no clear proof that the Benoits had committed mass murder. He'd based his ideas on the Benoit girl's story and on his own theorizing. Later, the pond, Wild Cove Pond, was dragged from end to end and across several times, but again the law found nothing. That was not to be wondered at as the water was reported to be deep and the bottom muddy and soft. Then over three years had gone by since the *Flirt*'s crew disappeared. If human remains had been lying there, during all that time, they would in all probability, have been swallowed in the mud.

My father sent a detailed report of his investigation, including Agnes Benoit's statement, to Inspector General Carty who in turn passed it along to the Minister of Justice, with the result that Magistrate Howorth was instructed to conduct a preliminary enquiry to determine if there would now be sufficient evidence to try the Benoits on a charge of murder.

The magistrate decided that there was and he committed them for trial which would take place in the Supreme Court in St. John's. The brothers, under a police escort, were brought to St. John's on the coastal steamer, *Curlew*. Agnes Benoit was brought along also, as she was considered to be a key witness. Mrs. Benoit was never brought to St. John's as although she maintained a friendly attitude toward the police, she insisted that she had no evidence to give against her sons. Reasoning therefore, that she would remain silent on the witness stand, it was thought unnecessary to subpoena her.

A brief note in the newspaper *Ledger,* dated September 25, 1877, read: Steamer *Curlew* arrived on Saturday last. Benoit prisoners returned by *Curlew* now in custody in St. John's Penitentiary.'

I dug through all newspaper files from 1874 to 1879, but apart from a short note in one paper which stated: 'Captain Fredrick Rideout was shipwrecked at Wild Cove, he and his crew are supposed to have been murdered by their guides.' I could not locate further details. Nor can any Supreme Court records of trials be found covering the period from 1877 to 1879 inclusive. It is possible that those records may have been destroyed in the great St. John's fire of 1892. So I can only set forth the remainder of the story as I'd heard my father relate it on more than one occasion. He said that he was the first witness called and he told of conditions as he'd observed them at Wild Cove.

He then commenced to advance his own theories as to what had occurred after the *Flirt*'s crew had come ashore. But the lawyer for the defense raised a strong objection to this. His objection was upheld by the presiding Justice. Incidentally, I never did hear him mention the name of the trial judge, nor the names of the lawyers for the prosecution and defense.

Agnes Benoit went into the witness box next and told her story almost word for word as she had recounted it to my father. He said that the lawyer for the defense gave the girl a very rough time during his cross examination. He screamed, stamped his feet and pounded on the desk with his fists. His purpose in acting in that manner was evidently to scare the witness, with the hope that she may slip up somewhere. At one point he shouted, "You miserable, little streal, don't you realize that you are deliberately trying to put a rope around the necks of your father and uncle?"

Here the lawyer for the prosecution objected to the innuendo used and to the suggestion made by the defense lawyer. He was upheld by the judge. If the defense lawyer imagined that he could make Agnes Benoit shiver with fright and by so doing cause her to change her story, he was sadly disappointed, for she remained calm and composed throughout all his ribald questioning.

She would reply, "It is like I told you just now. I saw my father and my uncle dig up one poor man, another poor man and so on."

To counteract the girl's story, there was the evidence of her father and uncle, who stated that they had never seen Captain Rideout and his men, so it would have been impossible for them to be the murderers. Another strong point in the favour of the Benoits was the fact that no item from the ship nor any article belonging to a crew member had been found in their possession. In addition, the crown had failed to produce a corpus delicti. Then again, Gil Benoit stated that his daughter was crazy, that any story she told could not be considered reliable.

The law proclaims that a person must be considered innocent until proven guilty. In such cases the burden of proof rests with the crown. Furthermore, a jury has to be convinced beyond a reasonable doubt that a person is guilty of the crime with which he is charged. The facts which I stated just now would be sufficient to cause doubt in the minds of any jury. For back in the 1870s persons convicted of murder were usually sentenced to be hanged by the neck until dead. In the Benoit case, a jury could hardly be expected to render a guilty verdict from the evidence they had heard and the doubts which had arisen. Possibly they felt that they would be condemning to death innocent men. So the verdict was not guilty and the Benoits were once more released from custody. The authorities obviously felt it inadvisable to return Agnes Benoit to Benoit's Cove. An R.C. priest very kindly volun-

teered to take her in, to give her work as assistant house-
keeper.

Just how long she remained in St. John's I have no way of
knowing, but in 1919 I was talking to a lighthouse inspector
named Field. He said that Agnes was running a boarding
house back in Benoit's Cove and that he had boarded there a
short while before. He said also that her uncle Exavior had
died several years previously, but that her father, Gil, who
appeared to be about ninety years of age, was living with her.

In August 1879, my father was transferred to Bonne Bay
to establish another new police district. Meanwhile, the rela-
tives of the missing seamen gave the Department of Justice
no peace. They continued to demand that a further investi-
gation be made as they contended that not enough had been
done to solve the mystery. The Department of Justice finally
bowed to this pressure and Head Constable John Sullivan was
ordered to proceed to the west coast and make a fresh start.

I would like to mention here that the rank of head
constable in the Terra Nova Constabulary back in those days
meant that the officer holding it was one step ahead of full
sergeant. The rank of district inspector, a rank higher than
that of a head constable, was not created until Charles H.
Hutchings took over command of the force in 1918. It
expresses the fact that Head Constable Sullivan was in the
number three position in the Constabulary in 1879. It would
seem that poor Mr. Sullivan was always called upon to solve
mysteries in areas where other law officers, including his own
heap big chief, Inspector General Carty, had failed. After
Head Sullivan completed his investigation and had returned
to St. John's, my father arrived in the capital from Bonne Bay
with a prisoner who'd been committed to serve a term in His
Magesty's Penitentiary.

Shortly after his arrival, he met Sullivan and asked him if
he had discovered anything new respecting the Rideout
disappearance.

"No," replied Sullivan, "the only thing I found at Wild Cove was the shin bones of a skeleton sticking up out of the sand, probably the frame of some old Indian who died there a hundred years ago."

My father said nothing, but he couldn't help thinking that those shin bones might have been all that remained of Captain Rideout's man, number twenty-one. Twenty-one men disappeared off the face of the earth, but Agnes Benoit was very definite when she said that she saw just twenty of those men being dug up. Provided that her story wasn't true, what could have caused such a comparatively large number of human beings to fade out of existence without leaving a trace? I assume it would seem silly of me to suggest that they simply melted into thin air, but would it? For it has been reliably documented that people have vanished even before the eyes of others who were watching them.

Orion Williamson was a farmer living near Selma, Alabama. One day in July 1854, he left his chair on the farmhouse porch and was crossing a field to bring his horses in from pasture. His wife and his children watched him from the porch he'd just vacated. Two of his neighbours, who were riding by, waved to him; Williamson waved back, then he vanished, suddenly, right in the centre of his field. Although no hole was discovered in the earth where he'd disappeared, relatives, friends and neighbours thinking that he had fallen into an underground cavern, tore up the ground and dug deeply all over the place. They found no caverns. Bloodhounds were brought in and they quartered about with noses to the ground, but they were no more successful than the humans. Farmer Williamson was never seen again.

The mysterious disappearance of one individual in such a manner must have been uncommonly startling, but how about it when a large body of troops vanish in a similar fashion? During the Spanish War of Succession, four thousand soldiers while marching through the Pyrenees, just faded away. In 1858, six hundred and fifty French colonial troops, on a march toward Saigon, disappeared fifteen miles from that city. And as recent as 1939, 2988 Chinese soldiers stationed south of Nanking, vanished. They left their camp in a perfect state of order and all their rifles were neatly stacked. Numerous cases of people suddenly and mysteriously disappearing have been reported from all over the globe. But why they vanish and where they go has not yet been determined.

To return to Captain Rideout. It would be naive to suggest that the men became so deeply depressed when no ship turned up to rescue them, that they committed mass suicide. One or two men might have taken that way out, but certainly not all hands. Well, the mystery wasn't solved back in the 1870s and no light has been thrown on the scene over the years that would account for the disappearance of the crew who'd manned the brigantine *Flirt*.

Finally at the risk of being accused of setting down words that produce tedious repetition, I feel compelled to emphasize that, despite the story told by Agnes Benoit and the theories brought forward by my father, Gil and Exavior Benoit must be considered innocent of committing murder, in that instance, for the jury's verdict read: Not guilty.

Final note on the *Flirt*: I located an item in the *Harbour Grace Standard* dated August 1875, which stated James Butler of Carbonear had purchased a new vessel to replace the brigantine, *Flirt*, which was lost at Wild Cove on the west coast in 1874.

Bibliography

Newspaper, *Newfoundlander*, St. John's: 1874 to 1879

Newspaper, *Ledger*, St. John's: 1874 to 1879

Newspaper, *Harbour Grace Standard*: 1873 to 1875

St. John's Evening Telegram: June 22, 1971

Newfoundland Stories and Ballads, owner/editor Mr. Harry Carter, St. John's

Strange Stories, Amazing Facts, New York: 1976

Celestial Passengers, U.F.O.'s, Space and Travel. Margaret Sachs with Ernest Jahn, Penguin Books: 1977